A Jealous God

Enjoy!
Dee Wilbur

To order additional copies, please contact us.
BookSurge, LLC
www.booksurge.com
1-866-308-6235
orders@booksurge.com

DEE WILBUR

A JEALOUS GOD

2006

A Jealous God

ACKNOWLEDGEMENTS

Thanks to:

Deborah Burks who always said we could and who read and typed.

Great readers: Anjali Salvador, Kay Dawes, Kerry McAuliffe, and Judy Adamson for reading early versions and for extra proofreading help.

Su Zanne Boone for reading many versions, early and late and making many excellent suggestions.

Pam Swingle for reading, editing, and proofing.

Roland Adamson of the George Foundation for his suggestions.

All the people at Booksurge: Thomas Kephart for directing the editing, Wade Tabor for the wonderful editing, Lynn Eang for being our main contact, Julie Burnett for the cover, Melissa Bolton, and Jessica Cornell.

The many others who listened, read, and gave us support, too numerous to list.

And especially Bryan and Sally for not disowning us.

For Bryan and Sally for Love

PROLOGUE

Richmond

Richmond, Texas, the location of this story, is an actual town located on the Texas Coastal Plains about thirty miles southwest of Houston. It is a small town of about eleven thousand souls. The county seat of Fort Bend County, Richmond was founded in the 1820's and incorporated as a city in 1835, ten years before Texas became a state.

Moses Austin had obtained the original land grants from the Mexican government allowing settlement in Texas, and his son Stephen F. Austin brought the settlers. The original three hundred settlers, known as the Old Three Hundred, received large grants of land on both sides of the Brazos River. The Brazos River flows through Richmond. Descendents of many of the Old Three Hundred still live in the Richmond area. The local cemetery contains the remains of Mirabeau Lamar, the second president of the Republic of Texas and the founder of the Texas public school system, Jane Long, the first white woman to give birth in Texas, and Erastus (Deaf) Smith, who had left the Alamo to tell the world of the Texans' plight. Change does not occur rapidly in Richmond. Richmond has had the same mayor for over fifty-two years.

Thompsons (originally Thompsons Camp) was an oil field camp about twenty miles south of Richmond and was the site of the initial oil discoveries in the area. At one time it had several hundred residents and its own small school. Only a few people still live in the area. Although a metallic building does exist at the end of a shell road across the railroad tracks in Thompsons, no toxic materials were ever manufactured there.

There is a large foundation benefiting the residents of Fort Bend County. It has funded many charitable ventures: the county library system, the county hospital, numerous parks, a large historical park, and an astronomical observatory. Many of the long time residents of Richmond are quite wealthy; their money is "quiet money" never spent ostentatiously but used discreetly to support worthwhile charities.

Many of the buildings and locations described in the book are real. The people are not; they are only figments of the authors' imagination.

CHAPTER 1

A low moaning sound woke him. At first he thought it was the wind. A "norther" had blown in, and the rain had started to freeze about sunset. But when he came fully awake, the moan sounded again, too low and too guttural for the wind. He turned and cried out, "Ann, what's wrong?"

"Something bad's happening. I don't know . . ." Her words were broken off by a piercing wail. Suddenly the lower bed was wet. "I think my water just broke. It hurts really bad . . . a bad contraction!" she gasped.

"You're only seven months. It's too early," his fear kept him from making any sense.

"I know it's too early, but I *am* having this baby," she said, grabbing her abdomen with both hands as another contraction hit.

Quickly Samuel got up, went to the bathroom, and grabbed a large bath towel. He stopped at her dresser and jerked out her blue sweat suit. "Here," he barked. "Put the towel between your legs and put on your sweats. We're going to Kerrville."

Samuel quickly pulled on his jeans and grabbed a flannel shirt he had dropped on the floor the night before. His boots slid on automatically. Ann had just finished dressing when he flipped her a pair of house shoes. "I'll get our coats."

He helped her on with her coat and then almost carried her to their SUV. Ann's whole body shook badly. He didn't know if the intense cold, the gut cramping fear, or the severe pain caused it. He shook too, making it hard to get the key in the ignition. He remembered the horror stories of deliveries gone wrong, and he started to pray, "Please, God, don't let Ann die!"

The nightmare continued on the drive to Kerrville. A deadly ice and snow mixture glazed the roads. His prayer became, "Please, God, don't let anything happen to Ann." He took his half of the road out of the middle. He made certain he kept the SUV on the road by keeping an equal distance between the fences along the roadside. Fortunately, he drove a four-wheel drive SUV with new all-weather tires.

A medical emergency had been one of Samuel's great fears of living in Leakey, Texas. The county seat of Real County had all the necessities for modern living: a courthouse, seven lawyers, a Mexican restaurant, a Dairy Queen, a real estate office, and cable T.V. It also had two filling stations, three churches, and 402 residents. The town boasted a brand new library. The school had grades K through 12 with forty-seven students in the high school. Ann wanted the same small town experience for their children as she and Samuel had had. But Leakey had no resident physicians, no dentists, and no ambulance services. Not what Samuel wanted for a pregnant wife.

Ann and Samuel had agonized over the decision to move there. Ann's uncle had died and left them what he called his hunting lodge. It was eleven cabins built around a pavilion and a swimming pool. With about six months of hard work, they had converted the lodge house into a restaurant and office with living quarters up above and had a ten-room motel. The area around Leakey was so beautiful that they had no trouble keeping the motel full. Samuel had filled the town's obvious need when he became the seventh attorney.

It took about two hours to reach the nearest hospital facility in Kerrville, on a clear day. A dentist visited once a month. An old G.P., retired from Houston to live in the Hill Country, came through once a month, bringing a crotchety retired R.N. with him. Samuel always thought it was just easier to be sick than face her.

Ann had seen the G.P. the week before, and he had given her the name of a new O.B. in Kerrville. Ann took the first available appointment for the following Monday. Ann didn't like going to doctors anymore than Samuel liked seeing the nurse.

Samuel almost cried in relief when he finally turned into the emergency room drive at the Kerrville hospital. He had called them on his cell phone as soon as he escaped the spotty coverage between Leakey and the rest of the world. As promised they had an attendant and gurney waiting at the door. As he climbed out, a large number of people began shifting Ann from the SUV to the gurney and then rapidly to a treatment room. Even though she had never seen the O.B. officially as a patient, he had agreed to come and was already inside waiting for her.

Samuel was shuffled off to the admitting desk. Things went very smoothly after he showed them a valid insurance card.

After two cups of machine-brewed coffee and what seemed like an eternity, Samuel recognized the doctor as he emerged from the treatment room. His face was grave, but his voice was full of kindness.

"Mr. Cox, your wife is going to be fine. The baby was born dead. The spine and brain did not fuse. The entire spinal canal was open to the outside. I'm sorry. We're going to take your wife up to the O.R. right now and do a dilatation and curettage to make sure that there are no remnants of the pregnancy or placenta left behind to cause trouble. You'll be able to take her home tomorrow around noon.

"I'll talk to you and your wife in the morning. As I said, the baby has gross abnormalities. I think you should send the baby's remains to the medical school in San Antonio. This would be important if you ever want to have other kids. I'll have names of doctors for you in the morning. I know that this will be rough for you both. I wish I could help, but mental and emotional problems are sorta out of my area. You both may need some counseling. Talking to your minister may help, too. I can handle your wife's medical needs. So now I'm going to the O.R. to take care of those."

"Do whatever you think best, Doc. And, thanks for coming. I know it'll be rough, but Ann's tough. We've got a good marriage and two healthy kids to love. We'll make it through. When can I see her?"

"Probably in about an hour and a half. Someone will come and get you here and bring you to recovery." The doctor headed down the hall.

"Thank you, God, for getting Ann and me through this. And, God, bless the soul of that little one. I never even got to meet him." Tears ran down Samuel's face. Samuel sank down in the chair trying to focus his thoughts on what he needed to do, who he needed to call. He looked at his watch; it was only five thirty. Only five hours or so since Ann's cries had awakened him.

"I've been throwing up every morning for a week," she said softly.

"Oh my God, you're not. . ."

Rachel interrupted before she could finish.

"Yep, in the olden days they would have said the rabbit died. Now it's your pee turned the stick the wrong color. I'm pregnant!" Rachel glanced over at her best friend's surprised face. They had been friends since the sixth grade. Rachel didn't know what she would have done without Dianna.

"But I thought Brad had a vasectomy?" Dianna asked, not really wanting to know the answer. She didn't feel like moral support. Did moral support remind the supportee of her morals? No, probably not. Dianna took a shut up and listen approach.

"He did, and no the knot didn't slip. You know our marriage has been pretty shaky since I discovered he was porking his bimbo secretary. He fired her and promised he'd do better. Well, three months ago my high school class had its reunion, and he wouldn't go with me. Ernie Schulze came to the reunion. You remember him. Good looking but geeky. They always said he was the biggest dick in our class . . . both personality-wise and anatomically." Rachel was calming down as she talked. Maybe Dianna's approach was working.

"They were right. Well, after four drinks, he really started looking good. We left the party about ten, went to his motel room, and fucked all night long. And size does matter." Rachel said, trying for humor.

"I feel like such a slut and a fool to boot. You know I'm Baptist," she glanced over to see her friend not looking at her. "So, an abortion was hard to think about. And I haven't even started dealing with the adultery issue, or maybe I have.

"I guess I still love that bastard Brad even though he can be a real jerk. I guess I'm not one to talk." She eased the car into a parking spot in the high-rise garage. When she had parked, she turned to face her friend. "Anyway I decided to have an abortion, and you've got to make sure I go through with it. You don't have to come back with me to see the doctor, but you have to make sure I don't jump up and run screaming from the waiting room."

"Oh, Rachel. Are you sure? Have you thought this through?" Dianna asked, taking her hand and looking at her squarely.

"Brad left this morning for a four-day business trip to California, so he won't be home until Friday evening. I should be back to normal by then. If not, I'll tell him I'm having a bad period with cramps. That usually shuts him up. Yeah, I think I've thought it through," Rachel answered, effectively dodging Dianna's real question.

They got out of the car and headed for the elevators. Just before the elevator arrived, Dianna said, "Rachel, when you called and asked me to come with you to the doctor I began imagining all sorts of things – plastic surgery, cancer, and everything in between. Well not everything – this never crossed my mind." She took a breath and then continued, "But I love you. I'm here, and you'll get through this. We'll talk more later, but you'll get through it."

They got on the elevator and silently rode to the sixth floor of the professional building. Dr. Norton's office was strangely empty, and Rachel went right in. After disrobing, she put on what she always called "the designer gown" and crawled up onto the table. The nurse rolled in a machine with what looked like a T.V. screen on top. She very professionally covered Rachel with the sheet while pulling up her gown.

"We have to determine the age of the fetus. We do not terminate pregnancies if the fetus is more than twelve weeks along. I'm going to do an ultrasound on your pelvis. The doctor will examine the ultrasound to see if we can proceed," she said.

They had told Rachel to drink a quart of liquid before she left home and to leave her bladder full. She thought she was going to explode. She wondered if leaving Dianna in the waiting room reading magazines was the best choice. She could stand someone to hold her hand and let her bitch.

The nurse squirted some warm gel on her lower abdomen and began rubbing it with what she called a probe. The pressing wasn't helping her full bladder at all. The probe was connected to the T.V. screen by a cord. Instantaneously a black and white image appeared on the T.V. screen. Thankfully, Rachel could not make sense of the image. "I'm going to take pictures of each of these screens with some electronic markers so we can determine the length of the pregnancy." After a few minutes of picture taking, she left the room. She returned in less than a minute with Dr. Norton in tow.

He looked very intently at the screen. After two or three minutes, he said, "Empty your bladder, get dressed, and come to my office. Did you bring anyone with you?" Rachel nodded, "Yes."

"You can bring them back with you."

Rachel said, "I'd rather come by myself." Rachel knew something was wrong. *Oh, God,* she thought, *I hope it's not twins.*

In his office, Dr. Norton was sitting behind his desk with a very grave look on his face. "Rachel, even if you had not come to have this pregnancy terminated, I would have advised you to do so. The fetus is grossly deformed. I don't know exactly what the syndrome is, but I don't think it is compatible with life. We'll schedule you in the morning and remove the fetus. You may have nothing to eat or drink after ten tonight. You're only eleven weeks along so there should be no problems. Nurse Jones will make all the arrangements. I'll want to send the fetus for study to the medical school so we can pin down exactly what's going on."

He reached into a drawer and handed her a pamphlet. "I am required by Texas law to give you this brochure explaining abortions. You may read it if you wish. Do I need to talk to your husband?"

"No, doctor, my husband must never know any of this," replied Rachel weeping softly.

CHAPTER 2

*D*amn it. Damn it to Hell!* thought Emma as her menstrual cramps began in earnest. She had been two days late and was hoping against hope that she was finally pregnant. Emma had succeeded in everything she had ever attempted . . . except getting pregnant. She was on partner-track at Houston's largest and most prestigious law firm. She was the tax group's rising star. Tax law suited her well. She liked knowing the rules, knowing what was black, white, and grey. She lived to make as much of the grey work as white for her clients.

She owned a house in West University Place, Houston's version of Yuppie Heaven, with her husband Bill Anderson, who was well on his way to becoming a partner with another large Houston law firm, the second most prestigious firm in the city. He was not ahead of Emma, but on track. West U., as it was known to its citizens, posted notices for the city council meetings, along with the agenda on the city's website. It was a very family-oriented, self-contained city nestled snugly within Houston.

Emma cursed again when she remembered how sure she had been that she could talk Bill out of kids. In their entire marriage, all seven years, having kids was the only disagreement that she hadn't resolved in her favor, she remembered. When they began looking for a house they both agreed on West U., but Bill thought he wanted a stucco house. She wanted red brick.

She also tried saying that stucco wasn't appropriate for Houston. Bill countered by asking how the River Oaks County Club house, the most prestigious country club in town, could be inappropriate? Then, because he knew he had her at a disadvantage, he mentioned

Bayou Bend, the premier house museum for American antiques anywhere: "Is Bayou Bend stucco?" he asked.

Changing her approach she talked Bill into the red brick by only showing him ugly stucco houses. Several of the houses they had visited with the realtor had mildewed badly. In the end they had moved into a lovely two story red brick home. *Oh,* she thought, *why did I have to lose the one point where I couldn't give in gracefully?* Since she had admitted defeat about two years ago, she had been trying to get pregnant; still no luck. As soon as she admitted that Bill wouldn't budge, she quit even pretending to drink the occasional glass of wine. She began taking a multi-vitamin with folic acid because if she was going to do something, she was going to do it right. They had been trying to get pregnant for over two years, and still no baby. Time to get some help.

With her usual head-on approach, Emma called the office of Dr. Chester Wornat, an O.B. fertility specialist suggested to her by one of the legal secretaries who had had a similar problem and now had a two-year-old son. After mentioning her co-worker and giving her address and insurance information, Emma was able to secure the earliest available appointment, on Wednesday ten days later. Comforted by having taken a positive step, Emma returned to the brief she had in front of her. Her client, a paint manufacturer, needed to respond to IRS allegations. Really they needed someone competent in their tax accounting group, but they didn't have anyone and, where would she be if they did?

Dr. Wornat was in his mid-forties and quite nice looking. He was a rather distant figure who had apparently chosen this area of specialization because of the large fees he could charge for *in vitro* fertilization and for the money his lab made on the extensive testing done. In the past one would have called Dr. Wornat a physician for the carriage trade because of his social prominence. Scarcely a week went by that he and his wife were not mentioned in one of the society columns in *The Houston Post*.

Emma was ushered into his office immediately upon her arrival. Dr. Wornat rose from behind a large oak desk. Only her folder was on the desktop. He came around the desk and offered his hand. "Mrs. Anderson, I'm pleased to know you. I'm Dr. Chester Wornat. Please have a seat," he said, offering her a choice of two high-backed leather chairs. "Would you care for something to drink . . . coffee, tea, water, Coke?"

"Water would be fine." He returned in a moment with a bottled water wrapped in a cloth napkin.

"For our first visit, I meet only with the wife. On subsequent visits, I bring in the husband as necessary. Today I will take a comprehensive history and do a routine physical exam. As many insurance policies will not pay for my services, I require payment in cash or by check or credit card as you leave." *Not typical words for a doctor,* thought Emma, *but maybe he's not your typical doctor.*

"Now . . . I need your life story from birth to the present. I'll interrupt with questions as we go. I need information specifically about your family, any hospitalizations, medications, surgeries, any illnesses, etc. Your schooling, foreign travel, where you've lived . . . please, include all these." He had his Mont Blanc pen ready to record her history in the file.

"I was born in Richmond, Texas, a small town just thirty miles southwest of here. My father was a general practitioner with a very large practice. He died of a massive heart attack just after my second year in college. He had been in excellent health and had no warning. My mother is still alive. She is sixty years old. She is a chronic alcoholic and rarely leaves the house. I think she is probably also diabetic. They had a son born three years before me. He was killed in a car wreck. My mother was driving and flipped the car in a ditch. She was not hurt.

"I attended public school in Richmond and Rosenberg. For college, I attended Rice University here in Houston, majoring in biochemistry and statistics. I was a cheerleader in high school and college. I graduated *summa cum laude* and went to U.T. Law School in Austin on scholarship where I was on law review. After law school, I clerked for Wilson Sanders, chief justice of the Texas Supreme Court for one year. I then returned to Houston and joined the law firm where I still work. I should make partner in a year."

Dr. Wornat thought it odd that she had not mentioned her class rank in law school.

"Bill, my husband, was born in Richmond at Polly Ryon Hospital, the same hospital where I was born. There is only one, so that's not unusual. In fact my father delivered him. His father was a history teacher and baseball coach. The Andersons moved to El Campo before Bill started school and then returned to Richmond when we both entered the eighth grade. His father became head baseball coach, and Bill thought that baseball was the most important thing in life. We had a few classes together but never really dated. Our main contact came on the debate team. Bill did great research in the fall semester, but his interest waned during the spring tournaments when baseball conflicted. He did well enough in baseball to earn a full scholarship to Rice. He idolized the Rice baseball coach.

"During freshman orientation week, I decided I wanted Bill. Within a month we were 'a couple.' After my father died following my sophomore year, Bill and I moved in together in a duplex in the Village. We married right after graduation from Rice, and both attended U.T. Law School. Bill is the only sexual partner I've had. Bill worked at a YMCA in Austin . . . he loves kids and teaching them sports. When we moved back to Houston, he made sure we got a house near the park in West U. so he would have space enough to teach his son baseball and maybe football. He said that the lots were too small for sports in West U., the home of the upwardly mobile and politically correct." She smiled as she said the last part, but the doctor knew that it was partially a warning to him to deliver on the promise of his reputation. That was exactly what he intended to do, so it was no problem for him.

"As for illnesses, I haven't really been sick that much . . . the usual colds and flu. I guess I was immunized for most everything . . . mumps, measles, chicken pox, pertussis, tetanus, etc. I had my appendix out at age fourteen and broke my left radius tumbling when

I was sixteen. My dad paid for a 'boob job,' I mean augmentation mammoplasty, for my high school graduation present. I was too flat-chested."

"What about medications?" he asked, without looking up from his notes.

"Nothing but vitamins, especially folic acid the last year. And an occasional aspirin or Tylenol."

"Never birth control pills?

"No. I got a diaphragm fitted and never had any problem." She appreciated his direct style.

"How long have you been trying to have a baby?"

"We have been trying for about two years with no success. I can't get pregnant," she answered, knowing that so many women had problems later on, but she couldn't seem to clear the first hurdle. "I wondered if it could be a problem with Bill's sperm?" she asked almost hopefully. If it was, then he would have to drop the whole baby thing.

"How often do you have intercourse and what positions do you use?" The interrogation continued.

"We probably have sex at least twice a week. I suppose we've tried every position conceived of . . . but mainly I like to be astride him on top. Does position matter?"

"Usually not, we'll see." Dr. Wornat made a notation on the chart.

"How regular are your periods?"

"I've been late a couple of times in the past two years but never more than a couple of days."

"Have you ever had any pelvic disease or infection?"

"No."

"Have you had frequent urinary tract infections?"

"I had 'honeymoon cystitis' when we first moved in together . . . but none since."

"Have you had any exposure to toxic chemicals or irradiation?

"Not that I know of."

"How about travel outside the U.S. or Canada?"

"I've been to Europe twice: once on a ten day sweep of European capitals and once to Paris for our honeymoon. And I've been to Mexico three, no, four times, but always at a resort."

He pushed a buzzer on the wall and a nurse appeared. "Please take Mrs. Anderson into the exam room. I'll need to do a complete exam including Pap smear and trans-vaginal ultrasound."

"Yes, sir. Please come this way, Mrs. Anderson."

"And, Mrs. Anderson, I will need to see you and your husband next week. Please make your appointment before you leave. Tell your husband we will want to collect a semen specimen. We'll do blood work on both of you next time."

Emma changed into to an examination gown and climbed onto the examining table. *At least the gown was cloth and not paper,* she thought. Dr. Wornat did the most thorough physical exam she had ever had. Every opening was examined and probed. Every area was palpated. A stethoscope listened for sounds even in areas she had thought to be silent. After he finished, a technologist, a young Asian woman, rolled an ultrasound machine into the room. A probe coated with gel was placed in her vagina and moved about while the technician and Dr. Wornat concentrated on images on a monitor. They took multiple pictures. It wasn't particularly pleasant, but it wasn't terrible.

Finally after what seemed like an eternity, Dr. Wornat broke the silence. "I've seen enough. Mrs. Anderson, everything appears normal . . . both on the physical exam and the ultrasound. Sorry for any discomfort we caused you. You have a retroverted uterus, which means your cervix is slightly upwardly tilted if you are on your back. So your preferred position should be the one you use. And you appear to be ovulating from the right ovary. I don't see any cause for immediate concern. We'll see you and your husband next week." With that he turned and disappeared from the room.

As she dressed, she thought back over the discussions she and Bill had had on having kids. From the beginning of their relationship, he had always insisted that he wanted them. And he wanted more than one. She had tried suggesting that pregnancy would ruin her figure, and he replied that he knew she would be beautiful during the pregnancies, and they would work as a family to get her back in the shape she wanted. "Babe, you know I think you are gorgeous now and always," he had said, killing that argument.

She hadn't even gotten the 'having kids is a scheduling nightmare' argument off the ground. He had merely smiled and said, "You can schedule anything. Under your direction they won't need more than twenty-four hours to have the three day measles." No, he had meant what he said, he wanted kids. Emma tried to cheer herself up with the thought that if it came to having *in vitro*, maybe she would only have to go through one pregnancy. Yes, that's what she would hope for, one pregnancy two or three kids, and then get back on task.

That night she told Bill about her appointment. "You have to come with me next Wednesday at three. Dr. Wornat will talk to you. He'll also get blood samples from both of us and . . . he'll need a semen specimen from you."

"Oh, great! Now I get to jerk off into a jar! I hope that at least they have some good magazines to aid the process, or do you come back and help?" he asked with a leer.

"Please be nice. We need to know what's keeping us from getting pregnant. He's a fertility expert with a good track record. I'm sure he can help. You know it's what we both really want." She watched him carefully. Yes, it was still what he wanted.

Bill Anderson arrived at Dr. Wornat's office just as Emma sat down in the waiting room. Once again they were taken back immediately to the doctor's office. Where Emma had been impressed by the size of the desk, the wood paneling and the deep carpet impressed Bill. They sat down in the leather chairs for only a moment before Dr. Wornat arrived.

"Mr. Anderson, I'm pleased to meet you. I'm Chester Wornat. Mrs. Anderson, good to see you again. He stretched across his desk to shake Bill's hand.

15

"This afternoon, Mrs. Anderson, I'll take your husband's history while you are getting your blood work done. Then I'll talk briefly to both of you together. Then you may leave while I do a brief physical on Mr. Anderson. Then we collect a semen specimen and draw some blood work."

Dr. Wornat pushed the buzzer on the wall. The same nurse appeared and escorted Emma to the blood drawing station.

After they left, Dr. Wornat explained, "Mr. Anderson, I have already gotten a great deal of information about you and your wife from her. I need for you to briefly answer a few questions for me."

"Fire away."

"What is the state of your health in general?"

"It's good. I take no medications. I've never been hospitalized. I've been cleated a few times on the legs playing baseball . . . only twice did I need stitches."

"Have you ever had any urinary tract infections or prostate problems?"

"No."

"Any history of sexually transmitted disease in either your history or your wife's history?"

"Not that I know of. My wife ran pretty wild in high school. She was a Daddy's girl. She drove a red Corvette in high school . . . the school's colors were red and gray. In college she drove a blue Corvette . . . Rice's colors were blue and gray. I heard rumors that she may have been sexually active back then. I know she got breast implants when she graduated from high school . . . another gift from Daddy. Emma was queen of the Fort Bend County Fair . . . a big deal when we were in high school. Civic organizations selected their candidate and then sold tickets in the girl's name. The one selling the most tickets won. Emma's dad bought five hundred tickets and tore them up. The implants won't affect her ability to nurse the baby, will they?" Bill asked with a sudden show of concern.

"No, the implants shouldn't affect her decision. But let's get her pregnant first. Continue with her family history."

"Her Daddy did all this to compensate for an alcoholic mother.

Emma's mother was the great-great-granddaughter of one of Stephen F. Austin's Old Three Hundred. These were the original three hundred settlers in Texas in 1821. They got large land grants along the Brazos River. They were land-poor farmers until the discovery of oil in the 1930's. After that she became 'somebody.' She had land and money.

"She courted and married the handsome young doctor who had just come to town. Her family had always had trouble with the squeezings of the grape. Tales tell that during courtship, she and the doctor enjoyed a glass of wine with dinner. When they married, they had a martini when the doctor got home. Soon after dinner, she had another martini.

"Their first child, a son, died in a car wreck. Gossip has it that she had been drinking before the accident. Anyway, after the funeral, she began having two or three martinis before dinner. She cut way back when she got pregnant with Emma. After Emma, she began drinking much more heavily. Now she has Bloody Marys for breakfast. I don't think I've ever seen her sober.

"I didn't know the old doc very well, but I understand he was a really nice guy. I've been told that after Emma's birth, he began sleeping downstairs in his study. Throughout his life he never had more than that one glass of wine with dinner.

"Most people are surprised that Emma's mother is still alive. They all figure she had pickled herself years ago. Emma has always hated and resented her mother.

"Emma was practically reared by Angela, a Latina woman who works for Emma's mother. Angela is probably why Emma is such a devout Catholic. Angela picked out Emma's baptismal gown. She helped select Emma's prom dress and wedding dress. She taught her about boys and about menstrual periods. She shielded the doctor, never letting him know about Emma's smoking or staying out all night.

"Listen, I'm sorry! I rattled on and on."

"That's all right. The information is important. Have you ever been exposed to any toxic chemicals or irradiation?

"No."

"How active are you and Emma sexually?"

"We only have sex two or three times a week." Dr. Wornat smiled to himself and noted on the chart what Bill had said about frequency. "Somehow it hasn't been as good lately. Emma seems to feel a great deal of guilt because she hasn't gotten pregnant. She knows that I really want children, especially a boy. Sports have always been a big part of my life, and I want to teach my son how to throw a curve ball. In fact, I made it clear up front before we got married, that children matter a lot to me. At first I worried that Emma would try to change my mind, but recently she has accepted this. And, now she's found you. I'm not sure she wants kids as much as I do, but I think she's committed."

"Ah, Mrs. Anderson," said Dr. Wornat as Emma came back into the room. "I'm just ready to talk to both of you together. Good timing." He handed them a large white paper with an empty graph at the top and four empty columns below.

"Here is a model temperature curve. Notice the inflection point that occurs when you ovulate. Mrs. Anderson, I want you to start taking your temperature orally every morning before you get out of bed. Record this on the blank chart I'm giving you. You may have sex as you desire until the first day of your menstrual period. Then you are not to have sex until your temperature chart shows the inflection point, the rise of one to two-tenths of a degree. You then have twelve hours to have sex as frequently as Mr. Anderson is able. This cannot be put off no matter what your schedule is. Do you understand?"

"Yes," they both nodded.

"I want to hear back from you three weeks after the time of the inflection point. Mrs. Anderson, you may go now. Nancy will have the charges for you at the desk." She gathered her purse up and headed off to see Nancy.

"You know some people have compared my job to that of a rancher who wants to ensure that his herd has a good crop of yearlings. But I think of myself as Nero Wolfe, using my skills to produce a beautiful orchid," Wornat said to Bill.

"The nurse will take you for the specimen collection. We'll call with the results. After we finish with the collection, we'll do a brief physical exam."

"Doc," said Bill jokingly, "Do you have any magazines to aid the collection process?"

"No, we use DVD's. The nurse will ask your preference." *The Nero Wolfe analogy might be right – he seemed pretty remote or removed,* Bill thought.

Thirty minutes later Bill left the office. He never did like prostate exams, but the movies weren't bad, and Emma certainly couldn't complain since this doctor was her idea.

CHAPTER 3

The ritual began. Emma moved a small end table next to the bed. On the table she placed a small fluorescent desk lamp, a box of tissues, and a digital thermometer in one of those containers which holds the plastic protectors for each use. She had several sheets of labeled graph paper in the under-table drawer. There was a blue pen for recording the temperature in tabular form, a black pen for making the dots on the graph, and a red pen to draw the line connecting the dots. A straight edge assured straight lines.

Every morning at six, Emma would awaken, put the thermometer in a new sleeve, and take her temperature. After two minutes she would read the thermometer and mark the value in the proper column. At exactly six oh five, she would repeat the process. She would then mark the spot on the graph with the black pen and connect it to the dot from the previous day with a red pen. She kept reminding herself that she had to make every effort. If this didn't work, then Bill might let her reopen the *in vitro* discussion, but right now this was the plan.

Beginning with the first day of her menstrual period, the graph maintained a flat, straight line for twelve days. Then on day thirteen there was a definite rise, the full two tenths of a degree. She slipped quietly from the bed and went to the bathroom. She brushed her teeth and changed into a see-through lace teddy she had bought for this occasion. After putting on some of her perfume, she slipped back into the bed beside her sleeping husband.

Bill Anderson awoke, realizing that something was different. Then he became aware of the fragrance . . . Poison, his favorite. This could evoke passion in a corpse. Today must be the day. He slipped from the bed and brushed his teeth. "A little mouth wash and after-shave wouldn't hurt either," he said to himself.

When he returned to the bed, he noted that Emma had coyly pulled the sheet up about her neck. With a sly smile on her face, she watched Bill.

"O.K., woman! How do you want it?" he said in what he called his mock caveman voice, as he jerked the sheet away and then gave it back.

"Bill, I read on the internet that a woman is much more likely to get pregnant if she is seduced and engages in lengthy foreplay."

Beating on his chest, Bill said, "I thought that was what I just did."

Then very gently Bill bent down and kissed Emma on the forehead, the nose, and the lips. He nibbled at each ear lobe and kissed her neck. He kissed her deeply, passionately, with his tongue probing the recesses of her mouth. Her tongue entered his mouth, hot like coals, starting a flame that moved throughout his body.

Bill pulled back the sheet, and a shiver ran over his body. *My God, she's so perfect,* he thought. He looked at her honey-blond shoulder length hair, her perfectly formed breasts, and her gorgeous legs that, as he always said, "Go from the ground all the way to heaven."

He bent over, cupping her breast in his hand. He took her nipple between his lips, sucking while he brushed the tip with his tongue. He loved the feeling as her nipple became hard and erect against his tongue.

Then quickly Bill went down on her. With his tongue and finger he brought her to climax. The convulsion seemed to spread throughout her body, and she moaned loudly.

Bill rolled onto his back, and she went down on him, showing that her tongue and lips were as talented as his. She paused for a moment and said, "Remember not to fire until your gun is in proper position."

After a few moments, Emma crawled astride him. She rocked back and forth, bending low so that he could briefly suck on her nipples. Then the gun began firing, a steady stream that seemed to go on forever. The shudder of passion ran through both of them simultaneously. Bill's only thought was *Emma will do whatever is necessary to achieve her goal, and for once it really works for me.*

The battle continued the rest of the day, as often as Bill with Emma's expert help could reload the gun.

The call from Dr. Wornat's office the next week indicated that all lab values were normal. Bill's sperm were numerous and excellent swimmers.

"Emma, you know I'm too old for this much activity. A man hits his sexual peak at eighteen, and it's down hill from then on."

"Well, maybe I should get a high school senior. I hear that they don't know what they're doing, but they can do it all night long. Or we can give up, but if you want a baby, we'll stick to the program."

As much as Bill thought he would enjoy the trying, it was difficult what with the temperature charts and the frenzy of 'the best days.' Once, thinking to ease the tension, Bill suggested making love right after her period, during the flat part of the chart, well before ovulation. That's when he learned they were making a baby—not making love or even having sex. Emma wasn't 'wasting' any swimmers or effort when nothing could come of it.

Then Saturday it happened; or maybe it didn't happen. Emma woke up and took her ritual temperature. It suddenly dawned on her. It had been over five weeks since her last period; three weeks after what they had been calling their "One Great Day of Passion." She hadn't started. Was she? Could it be? She fought back elation; she had been late before and gotten her hopes up.

Emma raced to the bathroom and pulled the home pregnancy test kit from behind the sheets where she had hidden it. First collect the urine. Then the test strip. Then nothing, nothing, nothing . . . and then it changed color. She was pregnant!

She pushed the speed dial button for Bill's cell phone. After several rings Bill answered in a whisper. Emma blurted out, "Come home now!"

"We're on the fifth tee," Bill answered softly, again in a whisper.

"You want to come home now, Bill. Leave the cart, or whatever! Just get here." Emma shouted and pushed the End button.

About twenty minutes later, she heard the tires screech in the drive. The back door swung open, and Bill rushed in. "What's wrong? It better be important! I left a client without a cart and told the marshal to send one to him. My shoes are in my golf bag," Bill explained, looking down at his stocking feet.

Emma just smiled and handed him the pregnancy test. "It's positive!"

The smile on his face erased years of her guilt. "Oh, Babe, that's great." He spun her around and kissed her. "Just great."

They had the greatest spontaneous sex they had ever had. Emma even let Bill be on top. A great burden and the curtain of guilt had been lifted.

CHAPTER 4

Usually Daphne, her legal secretary, would make her appointments, but this one was too personal. Two months after her last period, Emma called Dr. Wornat's office for an appointment. The first available date was in two weeks.

For the first time, Emma had to wait to see Dr. Wornat. It was only twenty minutes, but on top of the two-week wait for an appointment, somehow it seemed like an eternity.

When she was called back, Emma was immediately ushered into a restroom for a urine specimen. The nurse took the sample and performed the pregnancy test while Emma watched. The indicator turned blue. Again, it was positive.

Dr. Wornat immediately came into the examining room. "Congratulations, my dear. You are pregnant." Emma felt very smug while Dr. Wornat gloated over his success. Coming to Dr. Wornat had been the right course of action. They had gotten a game plan, followed it, and things were working out.

Yes, things seemed to be working out in all areas of their life. She had known from the beginning how much Bill had wanted a son to follow in his footsteps . . . maybe exceed his abilities . . . with the proper early training, maybe even the major leagues would be possible. O.K. so maybe Bill wasn't totally up to her expectations . . . but they were both on track for partner . . . and he was good in bed. The firm certainly wouldn't hold against her the time she took off for the pregnancy . . . she could see the headlines "Law Firm against Motherhood" if they tried anything. Maybe she could tone up Bill's social skills a bit . . . even if he did work for the second best law firm in Houston.

Then she put on a gown and went in for an ultrasound exam.

Somehow the ultrasound probe in the vagina did not impart the same emotion as Bill. After the young lady had taken her pictures, she excused herself and returned with Dr. Wornat. He did not speak but intently watched the monitor screen. Once he took the probe himself, taking additional pictures.

Finally he spoke, "You may get dressed. Then stop in my office, and we'll discuss your exams."

Dr. Wornat rose from his high-backed chair as she came into the room. "Won't you have a seat? Could I offer you some juice or bottled water?"

"Water would be fine."

He returned shortly with a bottle of water in a napkin. Dr. Wornat let her finish a swallow before he started talking. "Your pregnancy test is positive." He placed the ultrasound images up on a view box so that both he and Emma could see them. "But I am worried about the ultrasound exam."

He used a thin pointer to indicate areas on the ultrasound pictures. "This is your uterus. This structure is the placenta which provides nutrients to the baby from your body. This black area is the amniotic fluid the fetus floats in. This structure is the fetus. The appearance of the fetus is what worries me. Specifically I don't know what is wrong, but I am concerned with the spine. I want you to get an MRI exam at the hospital. Schedule it in the morning and schedule an appointment with me at one the same afternoon. Please bring your husband with you to the next appointment. It might be well to have him accompany you to the MRI as it can be somewhat scary. Nancy will schedule your MRI and your next appointment and have your bill at the front desk." With that Emma was dismissed. Empathy was not Dr. Wornat's forte.

Nancy already had the hospital x-ray department on the line. "Will a week from Friday at ten in the morning work for you?"

"That'll be fine," replied Emma as she took out her checkbook.

Emma waited for Bill to come home before discussing the appointment with Dr. Wornat. She wandered around their beautifully decorated house, telling herself that the MRI would show that the baby was fine. She tried to read a paperback but couldn't concentrate enough to read it. She looked at the bleak, grey November sky. She missed the spray of pink from the azaleas in the back yard. She thought of pulling some files to work on tax preparation, but that was not appealing.

As soon as Bill threw open the door, he shouted, "Could they tell if it's a boy? How big is it?"

Emma, in the living room staring out the front window, started crying; as she moved to the kitchen, the tears did not stop. By the time she got to Bill, she couldn't speak; she could only make short whimpering sounds.

Bill put his arms around her. "What's the matter, Babe? What's wrong?"

Finally she quieted enough to say, "He thinks there's something wrong with the baby! He wants me to have an MRI. Please come with me for the MRI and then for my next appointment with Dr. Wornat."

"When is it?" he asked.

"A week from Friday at ten for the MRI and Wornat at one."

"Sure. I'll go. What did he say was wrong? Did he say whether it is a boy or a girl?"

"He's not sure. He thinks there is something wrong with the spine. That's why he wants the MRI. He didn't say if it is a boy or a girl, and I didn't ask."

She had never really been keen on the idea of a kid . . . you got big, and fat, and sick when you got pregnant. She also didn't look forward to the dirty diapers and the middle of the night feedings . . . but they were committed, and she always honored her commitments . . . but she hadn't envisioned something going wrong. . .

The curtain of guilt had again descended.

Emma had filled out a questionnaire about her medical history and any metal she might have in her body while Bill flipped through some outdated issues of *Sports Illustrated*. She then changed into a hospital gown after removing all her clothes. They even gave her paper slippers to replace her shoes. She met Bill in a waiting alcove. "It's gonna be all right. It's gonna be O.K., Babe." he said. Then they took her into the room with the MRI.

The young man who introduced himself as the MRI technologist used a very soothing voice. "This machine makes lots of very loud, very strange noises which is why we give you ear plugs. The opening you go through seems very small and claustrophobic, but it's actually plenty large. Some people like to wear eye shades. We won't offer you any Valium or such because you're pregnant. The MRI is perfectly safe for you and the baby. Lie very still, and the test will only take a few minutes. Here's the button to press if you just have to come out of the machine. You probably won't need it . . . but if you have to, press it and we'll stop the test. We send the results to your doctor. Any questions?"

"I guess not."

"O.K. Just remember to lie very still. Your husband will be with me in the control room over there."

The exam, while very noisy even with ear plugs, only took only a few minutes as the technologist had said, and Emma soon found herself getting dressed. Bill was waiting for her out in the hall. "So how was it? You O.K.? Want to get a burger before seeing Wornat?"

"It seemed to go O.K. I can't eat, but I'll watch you if you buy me a glass of tea. The exam was loud and kinda cold. Otherwise, it was fine." She was scared of what the doctor would say. Somehow she didn't have Bill's optimism.

Promptly at one, they entered Dr. Wornat's office and were ushered back to the doctor's office without having to wait. Dr. Wornat rose and motioned them to the two leather chairs. He made no offer of something to drink. "I have discussed your MRI with the radiologists at the hospital. We are all in agreement. Your fetus has what is called rachischisis . . . this is a failure of fusion of the neural tube. In the severe form, as seen in this case, the outcome is invariably fatal. Most affected fetuses do not go to term. A few may live a day or two. We advise termination of the pregnancy at the earliest possible time." His style with bad news was very direct. After the initial salvo, he gave them a minute to absorb the news.

Dr. Wornat then began an explanation of what he meant by a failure of fusion of the neural tube. As far as Emma and Bill were concerned he might as well have been speaking Greek, for Emma because of the shock of suggesting an abortion, for Bill because science had never been his strongest subject. He finally asked, "Any questions?"

Emma quickly asked, "What are the consequences of not terminating the pregnancy? What would happen to me? I'm Catholic and cannot have an abortion for any reason. Isn't there some other test that we can run?" She hadn't yet accepted the fact that there was something the matter with her baby.

Dr. Wornat said, "No, I don't need any more diagnostic tests. There is no reason not to terminate. Even if you were to carry it to term, it would not live. It will put an unnecessary strain on your body and perhaps endanger the possibility of your carrying a viable, normal fetus in the future." He was not accustomed to having someone question his instructions, even those given as suggestions. He expected wholehearted agreement. He didn't need a discussion of religion. Nothing was going to make the situation any better. It was best to get over it and move on. Nero Wolfe didn't keep imperfect orchids around cluttering up his greenhouse. Emma made eye contact with Bill . . . Where was his support when she needed it so badly? She didn't understand the entirety of the decision of becoming Catholic when she made it . . . but Angela had told her it was the thing to do. Now was not the time to try to re-think it.

"I will not have an abortion!" Emma said loudly, clutching his desktop. "I just explained that to you. What part of it didn't you understand?" Then she seemed to withdraw into herself. Emma thought, *All the damned pro-choice women want freedom of choice to end a pregnancy. Why can't I have freedom of choice . . . to carry the pregnancy? Was it only pro-choice if the choice was abortion?* "Bill, you've known from the beginning that I'm Catholic . . . I can't just take off my religion when it's convenient . . . it's not like a wool coat you shed in the summer. Bill, help me!" Bill took her hand from the desk and laid it on the arm of his chair. Then he covered her hand with his.

Bill and the doctor continued as if Emma's outburst had not occurred. Bill asked quietly, "What caused this? Was it something we did? Or didn't do? She took vitamins all along. Who is to blame?"

Dr. Wornat replied that no one knew the cause . . . the condition was so rare. "I've never seen a case in my practice. There is some thought that exposure to toxic chemicals, irradiation, and possible genetic recessives could cause rachischisis," he explained. "You both denied any exposure to irradiation and toxic chemicals. You're not cousins are you?"

Bill said, "No radiation, no chemicals, and no we're not kin. What does being kin have to do with it?" He continued to pat Emma's hand gently.

"People often carry genetic defects as recessive traits in their DNA. These don't show up unless they have children with someone who also carries the defect. These traits often run in families."

Pulling her hand away from Bill's, Emma slapped the desktop to get their attention, "I have to know what caused this, and who is to blame. If you don't know what causes this, how do you know it won't happen the next time? Was this why I had so much trouble getting pregnant?"

Dr. Wornat reached for a small card and his pen. He wrote the name Raj Singh, Ph.D. with a phone number. "This is the name of a geneticist associated with Baylor College of Medicine. He is the world's leading authority on this condition. I suggest that you call him for an appointment." He stood up, clearly signaling that the appointment was over.

"I want you to go home and think about this. Talk with your husband. I'm sure if you and your husband talk about this, you'll change your mind and come to the right decision. It's inevitable. Call me when you do," he said confidently.

"Even if you were to remain adamant about not terminating the pregnancy, you will still need to be followed during the pregnancy. Do you wish for me to continue to follow you?"

"Yes, I suppose so," responded Emma in a monotone.

"Nancy will make an appointment for you in one month and will have your bill ready at the front desk."

"Doc, I've got a question."

"What's that, Bill?"

"Is it a boy or a girl?"

"I really don't know. The post-mortem exam after the delivery will tell us." Even Bill was astonished at Dr. Wornat's crassness.

At home that evening after supper, Emma watched as Bill cleared the dishes. It was unusual for him to be helpful like this. Emma thought, *He's trying to be sweet.* She began to tear up, and then despite her best efforts, she began to sob.

"I'm sorry, Babe. I don't understand. I wish your daddy were still alive. He could always make sense out of things. Maybe he could help you see that you have to terminate this pregnancy. I know everything seems wrong . . . but when you get over this, we can try again . . .and . . ."

"How in the Hell can we try again when we don't know what caused this? How can we start over when we don't know who to blame? Who's gonna pay for all this?"

"Babe," Bill whispered softly putting his hands on her shoulders and rubbing the back of her neck. "You've got to talk to somebody . . . a counselor, a shrink, Hell's bells, even Father Whatshisname. You need help to understand what to do."

Emma pulled away from him and walked to the sink, "Are you talking about Father Fleming?"

Emma scraped the food from the dishes into the disposer.

"Yeah, Father Fleming, he understands a lot about this. He can tell you about the church's position when the health of the mother is at stake," said Bill.

"Yeah, an un-married man knows all about marriage and pregnancy. A lot of help he's gonna be. And anyway, it's when the life of the mother is at risk. And my life isn't at risk!" Emma turned on the disposer drowning out any response Bill made.

Emma spent the rest of the weekend in bed, in a stupor. She finally got up and showered Sunday afternoon. Bill tried to give her some space, attempted to get her to eat, but finally gave up and mostly stayed out of the bedroom.

Emma couldn't think; she couldn't accept the new truth of her life. She understood that she was pregnant, but when she tried to think about the problems, her mind skittered away like a startled kitten. Each time she tried to think about what would happen 'after' the pregnancy, her mind simply shut down. She dozed off, only to awaken and at first feel the elation that came when she remembered that she was finally pregnant, then the downward spiral would start again.

Bill was no help; worse than no help. He came in quietly trying not to wake her, and when he noticed she was awake, he offered food. What an idiot! She wanted to slap the shit out of him; how could she eat at a time like this? She couldn't even think. She was losing her fucking mind, and he wanted to know if she wanted bagels. She put her hand over her mouth to keep from screaming at him. Bill thought she was nauseous.

Here she was, losing her mind and Bill was walking around like everything was normal. When he finally caved in and kept his Sunday golf date, Emma was relieved. Then she immediately felt guilty; Bill was only trying to help, the best he could. But, if anything were going to get done, she'd have to do it. Just like she was having the baby, so she got to decide.

In the shower, with the warm water massaging her, Emma could think slightly beyond the immediate. As she shampooed her hair, she realized that staying in bed wasn't an option. She had had a terrible blow, and it was only to be expected that it would take some time to absorb it. She couldn't go into work this afternoon like she usually did when Bill was golfing, but she could get ready for tomorrow. She needed to keep herself together so that no one at the firm suspected that anything was wrong. She would deal with that later. Thank God she hadn't told anyone except Bill that she was pregnant. She was waiting for the all clear from the doctor. Good joke that, but it could work in her favor. Surely Bill had respected her wishes on that too, but who knew with men. She'd confirm what she had told him this afternoon. They needed to have a united front on this. She'd come up with a plan about who they would tell about the pregnancy and when.

No one, that's who they would tell about the rachischisis. Emma was coming to hate that word. She would figure out how to handle that later. Emma sat on the un-made bed in her bra and panties, her blond hair still damp, but towel dried. I'll need maternity clothes, but probably not for a while. I can work in the doctor visits at first without any trouble. Daphne, her assistant, knew that Emma and Bill had been working with a fertility doctor, so some visits were expected.

Emma realized that she didn't need to figure out what she would do 'after' the pregnancy right now. What she did need to figure out was how to handle the first trimester, and she needed to get a grip on the next couple of months.

As she tidied her bedroom, and put on a pair of chocolate colored jeans and a cream colored top, she thought back over Bill's questions. How had this happened? What caused it? O.K., she was starting to believe that the baby had rachischisis. Dr. Wornat would have checked before passing on this kind of news. Now that her mind was functioning again, she needed more answers. She found her purse and the card with Dr. Raj Singh's information on it. She made a note in her PDA to get an appointment with him at the earliest possible time. She'd make the appointment herself and leave Daphne out of it.

"Hey Emma! Are you and Bill going to the partners' Christmas party next Friday? They're really going all out . . . River

Oaks Country Club, a full orchestra, and a midnight breakfast with champagne," bubbled Grace, one of Emma's colleagues. "Have I ever got a date with a winner? Makes me hot all over just thinking about him." She plopped herself down in one of Emma's chairs.

"Yeah, we're going to be there. I have hopes of making partner next year or the year after . . . so we gotta be there. I certainly don't want Bill to become a partner before I do. So tell me about this guy who's got your juices flowing." Lately, Emma's first reaction was to guide the conversation away from herself.

"Well, he's an attorney from out in Richmond . . . never married . . . mid-thirties . . . heterosexual . . . and makes Mel Gibson look ugly. And I've got him all for myself." She ended with a sigh.

"Well, bring him around, and I'll see if he's worthy of you. I'm really burning up the copier with these appeals filings for that pharmaceutical manufacturer that we represent. Who knows what their accountants were thinking—strike that . . . they clearly weren't thinking at all with the initial filings. They had some really good profits and tried to keep it all, move it around. What's going on with your case load?" Emma guided the conversation away from the holiday festivities, back to work. She had had just about enough of the holidays, and it was only the first week of December. Any enthusiasm she had for the holidays had dried up in Dr. Wornat's office.

They drove up the circle drive in front of the River Oaks Country Club in Bill's Porsche Boxster S. All black with black leather interior, the car fairly oozed money and testosterone, and went well with his tux. With reluctance, Bill turned the valet key over to the long-haired young man and watched as he helped Emma from the car. He wasn't sure who looked better—his car or his wife. Both looked stunning in their black, Emma in a crocheted dress with beads, a plunging v-neck and swinging fringe that kept it from being too short. The hormones of pregnancy had augmented the size of her already large breasts. The valet seemed equally conflicted as he helped her out of the car . . . to focus on the nice cleavage view the halter top offered him or to check out the car. He ultimately decided that he would have time to enjoy the Boxster later.

As they stepped to the main entrance of the club, Bill whispered, "I thought the valet was going to trip, staring down your dress like that. He didn't drool on you, did he?" He laughed, "Seriously, you look great, Babe."

Bill enjoyed the appraising and admiring glances that Emma drew as they made their way inside. Emma had selected the gown for its effect. Emma knew that she was good enough as a lawyer to become a partner. She wouldn't "sleep around" to get the partnership, but given a choice, men usually will pick a pretty package over a brown paper bag . . . and most of the voting partners were men.

They picked up their table assignment. A low number . . . Emma took it as a good sign, portending an early offer of partnership. They found their seats, and Bill went to get Emma a ginger ale and scotch for himself. There was plenty of time to see and be seen before the first course was served. Emma sat at the table, trying to get in the mood to make small talk and get through the evening. Since she had decided not to tell anyone about her pregnancy yet, she hadn't had any excuse to avoid the party. In light of her plan for dealing with the pregnancy and for finding out who had ruined her baby, getting through the holidays was the first step. Now, she just had to make it through tonight without anyone realizing that she had many much more important things to be doing than listening to their latest shopping disaster.

Within minutes Grace breezed over to the table with a very handsome man in tow. He wore a midnight blue tux with a tie and cummerbund decorated with Frosty-the-Snowman images. The touch of whimsy made him even more appealing. Grace, in honor of her good fortune, was obviously a few drinks ahead of most people. There was a slight slurring to her words, "Emma Anderson, I'd like you to meet Jon Miller, the sexiest lawyer in all of Richmond, and he's mine tonight." Emma glanced at Grace's strapless silk dress— the red silk with a rose pattern imposed on it picked up the red of

Frosty's muffler. *A lovely cocktail length dress,* Emma thought *even if it doesn't make up for Grace's lack of curves. And look at her nails, the wrong color, and her hair, all wrong for her face . . . she probably did them herself.*

"Hello, Mr. Miller." Emma said extending her hand. "I used to be from Richmond. I sometimes think it's a good place to be from. I'm from Houston, now. I still do some tax work for the Albert Foundation." By mentioning one of Texas' largest private foundations, Emma hoped to establish her position within the firm. She watched Jon's face closely to see if he got the message.

"Very pleased to know you, Mrs. Anderson," Jon answered, shaking her hand while Grace hung possessively on the other arm.

Bill walked up at that moment and handed Emma her drink. "Bill, this is Jon Miller. He belongs to Grace tonight."

"Actually I don't belong to her. She's just rented me for the evening." Jon's smile took the cut out of the words. He and Bill shook hands.

Grace leaned over to Emma and whispered, "Your nose needs powdering and so does mine. Come with me to the powder room." They excused themselves.

"Well, is he as advertised? . . . isn't he the most gorgeous thing you've ever seen? He just sends shivers down my spine!" Grace gushed as soon as they stepped into the hushed pink powder room. She flopped down on the nearest sofa. Emma re-evaluated how many drinks she thought Grace had had. At first she thought that nerves and two quick white wines could have caused the slight slurring, but watching her move, Emma suspected that a couple of quick Jack Daniels and Coke might have followed the wines. *Great, a drunk, horny co-worker, just what I need,* Emma thought, not really getting in the party mood at all.

"Grace, come on, you've had too much to drink. He is nice looking . . . but not that nice. Get a grip or you aren't going to make it through dinner. You know that this party exists to let all the partners see all of the 'not partners' in a social situation. Have fun on your own time. This is business." Emma worried that simply being at the same table as Grace could mar her record, delay her partnership. *No, I'll probably benefit by the contrast,* she reassured herself.

Grace heaved herself up and glared at Emma. "You get a grip. Just because you are married and dead doesn't mean that I can't enjoy Jon." Grace stalked out unsteadily without powdering her nose.

Following her out of the powder room, Emma watched as Grace caught Jon's left arm and spun him toward the dance floor. "Let's trip the light fantastic, fantastic one." Jon waved a feeble good-by to Bill and put his arm tightly around Grace. Bill didn't know if he was amorous or if he just thought Grace might be tipsy enough to fall.

"So what did you think of Barbie and Ken?" asked Grace as they joined the other couples on the dance floor.

"Bill seems like he's a nice enough guy. He's a lawyer, too." Jon had seen enough cat claws to know when to concentrate on dancing.

"Yeah. Emma sometimes calls him Avis. She says he works for the number two legal firm. She's real quick to tell you that she graduated *summa cum laude* from Rice while Bill only graduated *cum laude*. They both went to UT Law School. Must not be any difference in their class rank or we'd hear about that, too."

"Well, she's a very attractive lady," Jon said, noncommittally, but he wondered if maybe Bill hadn't graduated ahead of Emma from law school and maybe that's why she concentrated on undergraduate rankings.

"What's the matter, Jon? Ain't you seen 'store-bought' tits before? Her daddy got 'em for her high school graduation gift. That's what's so funny about Barbie and Ken Anderson, they really are plastic." Jon thought to himself . . . *With her blond shoulder-length hair, those store-bought boobs, and that black dress . . . she may be a doll but not Barbie . . . I think I'm too old for this Rent A Date shit even to help a friend.*

After three more drinks over the next hour, Grace was falling asleep at their table. Before anyone at another table noticed, Jon gently steered "Sleeping Beauty" to his car.

"Bill, what's in the box?" Emma asked as they were finishing their buffet meal, after Jon and Grace had made their exit. The other couples at the table were dancing. Bill had brought a box the size of a large shoe box with them. It had been sitting on the table the whole evening.

"Emma, you know how I love the Statler Brothers, and you know that they just retired from touring. Well, they're having a sale of all the memorabilia that they've accumulated in their store over the years. I bought an almost complete set of their Christmas tree ornaments over the internet, and they came today. They've been putting them out every year for fourteen years. They'd sold out of 'Year One.' I think they'll be cool on the tree this year." Bill was obviously pleased with himself.

"Bill, I don't think I can face Christmas this year. I ordered a hundred cards with the firm name printed on them . . . I couldn't bring myself to sign them . . . 'Oh, tidings of comfort and joy' seemed like bullshit. I made Daphne sign and address them." Emma wondered what Bill thought was going on with them. She was at the beginning of what would have to be a horrendous experience, giving birth to a baby who would die immediately, if not be born dead; and he was out buying Christmas ornaments.

"Come on, you know how I love Christmas. Don't you think just a little Christmas spirit might cheer you up?" Bill asked.

"No, I don't. And don't start whining; if you want a fucking tree, you can get it yourself. Every day when you come home, you can go through the mail and select any cards you want to open. The rest I'm gonna take to Angela to let Mother open. She gets a real kick out of opening mail even though she can't remember the names of any of the people.

"Oh, yeah. I don't think New Year's Eve is gonna be a bright spot either this year," Emma added. Bill glanced at the dance floor but restrained from suggesting they dance. Better to just keep his mouth shut and hope to get home in one piece. He concentrated on being the perfect corporate spouse, smiling and nodding.

Jon drove up to Grace's condominium, and taking a key from her purse, let both of them into the living room. A floor lamp provided enough light for him to make his way to the bedroom. Jon pulled back the covers and laid Grace on the bed. He removed her high heels and then covered her with a quilt. Sleeping in it wasn't going to do her dress any good, so he rolled her on her side, slid the zipper down and had the dress off of her in nothing flat. At least he wasn't losing his touch. He tossed it gently on the bedroom chair. He kissed her gently on the cheek and backed out of the room. He locked the front door and dropped the key through the mail slot. "Sweet dreams and Merry Christmas," he muttered as he drove toward Richmond pretty disillusioned with big time law practice in Houston.

Monday at the office the phone rang before Maureen, his secretary, arrived. "Jon Miller here."

"Jon, I'm so sorry. I apologize," sobbed Grace.

"What are you apologizing for?" He had expected the call but not the tears.

"For passing out Saturday night. I was just so excited, and I guess I just passed out."

"Well, it was a little embarrassing at the club, but you sure made up for it at the condo."

"What do you mean? What did I . . ."

"You don't remember? Man, it was the greatest I've ever had. You can do things with your tongue that ought to be illegal. In fact, thinking about it, I think they are. Can I call you in a day or so? Maureen, my secretary, is flashing me the distress signal on the intercom."

"I am so sorry. I feel like such an idiot. I can't remember a thing."

"Don't worry. It was great, and I'm sorry, I must not have made much of an impression on you; not what a man likes to hear. Please, let me try again."

"Of course. Give me a call. I've got to get back to the grind. See you."

"Bye." Jon ended the call and worried a little about the white lie of Maureen needing him and less about the one he had told Grace.

CHAPTER 5

First thing Monday morning after the party, Emma made the appointment to see Raj Singh, Ph.D. at his office in the Texas Medical Center at Baylor College of Medicine. By checking the biography given in conjunction with papers he had published and looking at university records on Baylor's web site, Emma learned that he was born in New York state and got his undergraduate degree at NYU. Raj Singh had obtained his Ph.D. in genetics from Stanford where he had published several papers from his dissertation on the localization of specific gene sites. He had come directly to Baylor and was now an Assistant Professor in the area of Developmental Medicine. He had a fairly open schedule, and she was able to find an opening the next morning.

Emma found him sitting in a small, cubbyhole of an office in one corner of his lab. "I'm Emma Anderson, and we spoke on the phone," she said to alert him of her presence. Through her research on Dr. Singh, Emma had learned about his academic background but nothing had prepared her for the man himself. He was a tall, handsome man. Emma found him dressed in a blue t-shirt, scruffy blue jeans, and run-down Nikes. There were knots in the shoe strings. Even though she had worn one of her plainer outfits, Emma still looked nice enough to go to her office if necessary . . . but she was really over-dressed for this appointment. She wondered if Singh would notice the contrast between her clothes and his. Somehow she doubted that he would.

The lack of financial reward for the work was one of the reasons Emma had changed her mind about medical school mid-way through college. Her mother and father had never co-mingled their monies. When he died and Emma probated the estate, Emma saw how little her father had in the way of a separate estate . . . and Emma liked the things money could buy. She knew that she would inherit all of her mother's very large estate that she currently managed, but she had wanted money of her own until that day. Now she thought, *I'll have to find some legal way not to co-mingle mother's estate with Bill's money. Unless you have a practice like Dr. Wornat's, it's easier to make the big bucks as a lawyer.* Emma even resented the things her dad had given to the community and especially the foundation he set up to help provide medical care for indigent children. She could have put the money to better use.

"Ah, yes, Mrs. Anderson. How may I help you?" Even though he had been reared in the U.S., he still had the English accent and a slight lilt heard in many from India, undoubtedly a gift from his parents. Books covered the desk, the shelves, and the floor. Dr. Singh moved the books from a chair in the corner and indicated that she should sit there.

Emma told him of her situation. "I heard that you are a leading expert on this condition, and I want to learn more about it. I want to know what caused it. If it is a genetic problem, what causes that? Who is to blame? Can it be treated? This is all I can think of. I can't concentrate on my law practice. The guilt is ruining my marriage.

"My husband wants a boy so bad . . . I'm afraid he'll stop loving me if I can't give him a healthy one."

"Ah. That is where you westerners have it all wrong. Love has little to do with a good marriage. When I get a little older and am ready for a wife, I will tell my mother. She and my father will find a suitable young lady and talk to her parents. It will all be arranged."

Emma ignored Singh's ludicrous statement about arranged marriages and continued as if he hadn't spoken. "Perhaps if I could talk to some other parents who have this problem, we could form a support group and help each other. I understand that you keep a registry of known cases in the U.S . . . maybe you could give me the name and address of some of these people, and I could talk to them."

"I cannot understand why you Americans always want to talk about your problems with someone else. Federal law prohibits me from divulging any names or information about patients."

"Look, I've got to get some understanding of this problem. Is it a disease? A condition? Or what? I rarely drink and certainly haven't had any alcohol since we've been trying to get me pregnant. I'm down to one diet Coke a day and no coffee. I've been taking a multivitamin with folic acid for years. What causes this? Who did this to my baby? Who ruined my baby? Is it caused by the mother or the father?"

Emma looked away from Dr. Singh and tried to regain her composure. She took a deep breath, "I'm sorry, Doctor. Let's start again. I would like more information about what causes rachischisis, and Doctor Wornat said you could help me with that. Do you have journal articles I could read? Are there books? I started out as a pre-med student at Rice. I ended up getting a degree in biochemistry, and I took a lot of statistics. So I should be able to understand your explanation. I went to law school when I figured out that my interests were really more in the legal area." *And I realized that as an attorney I would make a lot more money and wouldn't have nearly as much governmental intervention and regulation,* Emma thought smugly. *After Dad died, there wasn't anyone who cared what I majored in except me.*

"As you understand, rachischisis is a fatal, pre-natal condition," he continued looking pointedly at her mid-section, "that is caused by a defect on the thirteenth chromosome. I'm very close to determining the exact location." Emma was taken aback by his frank perusal of her body, especially the fact that he slighted her trophy breasts where some men directed their entire conversation and attention.

"Dr. Singh," Emma began to move away from the discussion of her specific pregnancy.

"Please call me Raj."

"O.K. Raj. I'm Emma. This defect on chromosome thirteen, what causes it?"

"That's harder to say . . . many of the same causes as other chromosomal damage, chemical exposure, chemotherapy, irradiation, etc. The root cause of your problem is unlucky pairing. You obviously do not have rachischisis. Your husband doesn't either. I know because you are both alive and over a week old. But you are both carriers for this trait. Or more precisely, the father of the baby and you are both carriers."

Emma ignored the reminder of the outcome of her pregnancy and focused on the information that Raj was giving her. "Raj, I've read that about one in six hundred babies are born with Downs syndrome. What are the numbers for rachischisis? And, by the way, my husband is the father."

Raj thought for a moment, "The incidence of spina bifida which would be at one end of the spectrum of this entity is one point five to two per one hundred live births in the U.S. A more pronounced form of this could have an incidence of one in ten thousand births. Something of the degree which your fetus exhibits . . . maybe one in one million." His answer was delivered in his best professorial voice.

"I can tell you in Texas in the last two years we have had four reported cases, including yours. That is a very high incidence." Raj seemed reluctant to talk about specific cases or even much about her situation.

"So I shouldn't be expecting a call from the March of Dimes about establishing a rachischisis group," she asked, trying to lighten the tone. She failed.

"I have some reprints you may have. You won't find much in any textbooks. Can you really do statistics?" Raj asked, finally showing some animation. "My last paper was returned to me. The editors said that I had not handled my data correctly. I know the raw data is correct. If you could re-do my tabulations, I would answer all your questions as best I can. What afternoon can you work?" Emma smiled. She understood now what Dr. Singh's motivator was—publishing his work. And she was fine with that; she could work with that. She needed his explanations and access to him to find out, in her particular case, what caused this.

"I'll work on Thursday afternoon . . . after lunch. I'll need a computer . . . the latest version of Windows. I'll bring my own programs. Please find an article with similar data that was published where you want it to be published . . . also provide the submission guidelines. We need to see exactly what they are looking for." Emma was intrigued by the opportunity to look at Raj's data and by the very high incidence of rachischisis.

A month after she began working Thursday afternoons for Dr. Singh, Emma and Bill were reading in the den after dinner. Emma said, "It took me three Thursdays to determine that Dr. Singh's work had isolated a defect to the short arm of the thirteenth chromosome as a genetic recessive responsible for the neural tube fusion problem. Dr. Singh has not determined the cause of the genetic defect. He is evaluating the effect of exposure to toxic nerve gases and other chemicals." When she started talking, he immediately put down his papers to listen. Bill never initiated the subject of the baby, the pregnancy or her work at the lab, but he always tried to be receptive.

"It took me two Thursdays to find where Dr. Singh keeps the names and addresses of all the recent patients. I need to know about the other cases of rachischisis," she explained.

"Isn't that confidential information? Won't you get in trouble when Singh finds out you were looking at things you shouldn't be? And, don't those other people, even the dead babies, have some right to privacy?" Bill wasn't sure why he felt so strongly; maybe because Emma's behavior was starting to concern him. She had always been very compliant with rules. Or he thought she had. O.K., speed limits didn't count. But they didn't cheat on their income tax, did they? Emma handled all of that. What a disturbing thought. Bill brought his mind back to what Emma was saying.

"Yes, the information is confidential. And that's the problem now. The confidentiality is working to protect whoever caused this chromosome to mutate. Don't you want to know who caused this? I've got to see the data so I can understand the pattern and know where to look next." Emma glossed over Bill's concerns. She wasn't going to get caught—Singh wasn't smart enough for that.

"Speaking of data, it only took me thirty minutes to correct the errors in the data tabulation. He is a good clinician and collects good data. He has no clue as to how one statistically interprets data. He arrives at his conclusions by gut instinct. He interpreted correctly this time . . . but that method of interpretation rarely works.

"I've been thinking, we need to have our own copy of our DNA profiles. I'm working out how to get them."

"Why? What possible use would they be to us?"

"I want a copy that's not in our medical records so that it can't be used by an insurance company to deny us coverage."

"What are you talking about?"

"Dammit, you know how insurance companies are. Any little thing they can use to deny you coverage, they do. So I don't want this out there in case of . . . whatever." She had started to say in case I ever get pregnant again, but she didn't need to get into that argument right now.

The bigger she got, the worse she felt, the more she knew that she should have never let Bill manipulate her into this. Never again.

"And, I want Singh's technician to run the tests on us. Maybe we can see how much of chromosome thirteen is defective. I keep wondering now if those times I was late with my period if it was a very early miscarriage. There's more to this than anyone's telling us, and I'm gonna find out what it is."

"O.K., giving the sample for this test can't be any worse than the sperm sample, can it?"

"No, she just swabs the inside of your cheek. That's all. You don't even have to take off your clothes, and there are no DVD's for you to watch."

Dr. Singh was very fortunate to have Gladys Koeppen working for him in his lab. She was a lovely young lady of Filipino descent who had married an anesthesiologist from Houston. She had obtained her Master's degree from the University of Houston in genetics. Gladys was responsible for all the DNA analysis in Dr. Singh's lab. Emma made sure she and Gladys hit it off at once. Emma could spot a power base when she saw one. They shared talk about all the new fashions and which stores in the Galleria had the best prices even if Emma was less concerned about prices than Gladys was.

One afternoon as they sat sharing some tea sent by Gladys's mother from the Philippines, Gladys turned to Emma, "I know it's none of my business, but why haven't you terminated your pregnancy? At the present time, there is nothing that can be done for your unborn child. I know the thought of an abortion is hard to take, but I have heard Dr. Singh saying you should terminate. As hard as it may seem, it might be easier to remove this pregnancy and begin again. How does waiting help? My mother used to say that God alone can set the time for one's death—but not any more. And there's the recovery, no matter what- it just seems so hard, you're being here looking at all the results and just waiting."

"I know," said Emma, "but I'm Catholic, and Catholics don't terminate pregnancies. I don't spend a lot of time trying to put science and the church together, but it is what I've been taught. Funny how it's stuck with me. My husband wants me to talk to a priest, like a priest would understand."

"I understand the conflict. I'm Catholic too. It's a real bitch! If I can do anything for you, let me know. I try to balance what the church says with what I see. This is so sad watching you; it's like watching the end of a sad movie that you know is going to end in tragedy."

"Would you do a chromosomal analysis on me and my husband . . . without telling Dr. Singh?"

"No problem."

Emma and Bill came to the lab the next day at lunchtime. Gladys got the specimens. Emma picked up the results the next Thursday afternoon. *Now*, she thought, *I have the DNA profiles and the names of other Texas victims. I can begin the real work.*

Dr. Singh called Emma into his office, "I've got great news. My paper has been accepted for publication. The changes in the analysis of the data were apparently just what they were looking for.

"You're so smart about so many things. Why are you so stupid about this pregnancy? There is no doubt about the rachischisis; the ultrasound shows it clearly. Especially the most recent scan that Dr. Wornat did. Continuing the present course is idiotic.

"If you must cling to this stupid religion of yours, why don't you have an induced labor? Then you can pretend that you have followed the dictates of your God."

Emma didn't respond immediately. Then she said, "Look, I've cleared up your data. You don't have any more ways to run the data, and you don't have any new data. You don't know anything more about the cause of this problem in my specific case or about the seeming 'outbreak' in Texas than you did when I first came. So we're even! I won't be coming back. And I'm not stupid. Good-bye."

"Jon Miller, here."

"Jon, this is Sandy. Mardi Gras is early in February this year. Can you come?" The invitation was a bit rushed, but that was the only sign of her nervousness.

"I thought you'd never ask. Sure, I can come. Wouldn't miss it." Jon was grinning already.

"Will you be able to stay the whole week, like last year? I've cleaned the hot tub and bought one of those fancy air mattresses for the bed."

She didn't need to bribe him, but it was nice to hear. "I'll stay the whole week if we can go to the parade where all the gals flash you with their naked boobs. What do I need to bring?"

Jon's thoughts drifted momentarily back to the Christmas party when he first thought about closing up his "Rent-a-Date" agency. *Every sane man worried about the big commitment that marriage meant . . . but Sandy was certainly special . . . she was smart and good looking . . . she would fit right in with family . . . his nephew and niece would love her . . . and she would certainly fit in Richmond. Maybe this trip he could get a promise from her . . .* His reverie ended, and he came back to the conversation.

"We can go to any parade you want, and I'll flash my naked boobs at you whenever you ask when we're alone. I'll get you a costume. If you're driving, could you bring some champagne, you know the special kind you get at Spec's? You know the kind that makes me feel romantic?" Oh, yeah, Jon could do that. She continued, "The festivities last about a week, so I'll expect to see you on February 10. Rest up between now and then," Sandy said in a lightly teasing voice.

"I will. I've really been thinking about you . . . thanks for calling. I'll give you a call when I get my shit together, and we can make definite plans. I can't wait!" Jon wondered how he was going to get any rest thinking about spending several days with Sandy. The first distraction would be that night at choir practice.

Jon attended the Methodist Church in Richmond which had been founded in 1835 before Texas was a state. Some of the original families were still members, and some were new arrivals like Jon. The congregation had long outgrown the small sanctuary built in 1921, but strong emotional ties had defeated many attempted building programs. Cynics used the small size as an excuse not to attend church services . . . "It's always so crowded."

The choir had met every Tuesday night for practice since 1835 except when hurricane Carla hit in the early sixties and knocked the power out for a week. The choir, while very musical, was best known for two things: the degree of education of its members and the quarterly ethnic food and drink parties the group held. Only one person in the choir had not graduated from college. In the twenty-four person group, eighteen held advanced degrees. Jon fit in well and enjoyed the friendship and camaraderie as much or more than he did the cantatas.

The ethnic dinners had started out with a simple enchilada dinner with Mexican beer. The dinner moved from house to house every three months, and each member tried to out-do the previous affair. Everyone seemed to agree that the high point in the series was the stir-fry and sake party at the Melford's when everyone ended up fully clothed in the swimming pool. "The Old Rugged Cross" had been somewhat rugged the next morning.

Jon's parents were Baptist, Southern Baptist. When he grew up in Victoria, Texas, the cool kids all went to the Methodist Church. So Jon had joined the Methodist Church at fourteen, with his parent's blessing. Mama always said, "I don't care where you go to church as long as you go." He had kept that in mind.

When he moved to Richmond, Jon had visited several churches, Methodist and Baptist. The choir director at the Methodist church had buttonholed him after his first visit and invited him to choir practice the next Tuesday. Once he had met the group, he was hooked. He could truthfully answer 'yes' when Maureen, his secretary, had asked him if he had found a church yet. He hadn't been in the group long enough to have to host the quarterly ethnic dinner. His turn hadn't come up yet, and he suspected that the alto who coordinated the dinners hesitated to burden a bachelor. And that suited him just fine.

The night after Sandy's invitation, his mind wandered during rehearsal . . . *what did Sandy have planned?* Fortunately the musical program for the next Sunday only contained favorites so Jon already knew the words and music. He had enjoyed last Mardi Gras, and his visits since then, but he wondered if she was signaling a new phase in their relationship, and if she were, what did he think of that?

After two long and very distracted weeks and one Sunday when Jon added his presence but not his voice to the choir because he had dreamed through rehearsal and didn't know the music, the waiting was over. He had already taken Cato, his chocolate lab, to the office. He would be a guest of Maureen and her husband Gus during Jon's trip. About ten on February 10, he started the six-hour drive to New Orleans with a case of pink Tattinger's champagne, various consumables from Spec's, the largest liquor store in Houston, and enough clothes to last a week. Once he got through Houston, he would be going against traffic on I-10 and it shouldn't be too bad. He'd get to New Orleans about four, before the heavy evening traffic.

Some morning fog cost him about thirty minutes, but he made it up by judicious speeding. Whatever her plans about the future, Jon was ready for some serious revelry.

Sandy O'Rourke, the lady causing his distraction, lived in a garage apartment in the Garden District in New Orleans. This area with its old, stately homes and wonderful trees covered with Spanish moss was more than Sandy could afford on a teacher's salary. And private high schools paid less than the public schools, but the garage apartment allowed her to live in beauty within her budget. Jon had tried repeatedly to get her to move, even going so far as to propose marriage. She felt obligated to remain in New Orleans near her ill, widowed father. She wouldn't live with her father, but she would visit him daily. With teaching, one-on-one tutoring of students for the SAT and ACT, and taking care of her dad, Sandy was very busy. But she turned down all of Jon's offers with an "All in due time, Jon." Hopefully now was "due time."

Jon pulled his car up the long driveway into the spot beside the garage that he had used the year before. He drove a new, retro Thunderbird, purchased after getting his fee from his first really big settlement. It was Thunderbird blue, a real throwback to the original T-birds.

He was able to carry his bag and the champagne up the stairs in one trip. A note was stuck to the door, "If you brought the champagne, you can come in and put it in the 'fridge. Otherwise, just wait in your car. I'll be back in a minute."

"What a wise-ass! What a wonderful wise-ass!" He felt a surge of energy and a sense of expectation.

Jon put up the champagne and put his bag in the bedroom. He had also bought out Spec's. Recognizing that Sandy's finances were not of the best, Jon used his trips to stock her larder. Returning to the car, he brought in a ham that they could snack on for the whole week, some brie and stilton cheese, three loaves of fancy bread, and three bottles of Texas red wine. In addition, he bought a gallon of Wiederhehr Alpine Rose from the wine cellars located in Altus, Arkansas . . . for five dollars a gallon how could you miss? An

Arkansas wine from a Texas Guy for a Louisiana Miss: what more could she want? Nothing, Jon hoped.

The door suddenly flew open. "Who has broken into my apartment? Is it the mad rapist?" Sandy shouted.

Jon laughingly replied, "I'm not mad at anyone."

God, Jon thought, *she is so beautiful.* The last rays of the sun through the window made her red hair sparkle. She was tall, about five foot ten with a figure that stirred the imagination. She had fascinated Jon since they were both undergraduates, he at Tulane and she at Sophie Newcombe. He found her mind to be as fascinating as her body. She was quick-witted and had a wonderful sense of humor.

Sandy set the sack of groceries she was carrying on the table and turned toward Jon. She was wearing a dark blue sweat suit. With a quick motion she lifted the hem of the sweat top, exposing her bare breasts to Jon. "I told you I'd flash them at you whenever you wanted, and I thought by the look on your face that now was as good a time as any. What do ya think?"

"I think you're right! Hey, I brought one bottle of bubbly in a plastic sack with ice around it so we could get started early. Shall I pop the cork?" Jon walked over and kissed her, gently at first and then with greater passion. His tongue played over the top of her tongue and probed the recesses of her mouth. It was like a match on tinder. Passion welled up from the depths of their beings.

"Forget about the champagne for a while," she whispered. She unbuttoned his shirt and slid her hands over his nipples. She pinched both nipples almost to the point of pain, and then as if to spread a healing balm over them, she caressed them with her tongue. "Jon, I love you . . . more than you'll ever know."

He turned her away from him and pressed himself against her buttocks. Jon slid his hands under the sweats and began to caress her breasts. He bent down and kissed her on the nape of her neck. She responded with a soft purring sound. She moved her hands around to the front of his pants, "I don't think we need to fill the prescription for Viagra."

"Sandy, if you won't agree to marry me, at least give me the right of first refusal?" He hated to seem to beg, but this was important. He knew it was too blunt, but the words he had practiced on the way over seemed to have escaped.

"Done."

Jon pulled her sweat suit top off and paused to look at her. He bent down and began circling each nipple with his tongue. Then he began sucking and nibbling gently with his teeth. Sandy removed his shirt and undid his belt. She unbuttoned his pants and in one swift movement pulled his pants and his shorts to the floor. Jon kicked off his shoes and stepped out of his pants.

"I can't believe," she started, "that we're doing this in the kitchen."

"So I guess we better hurry, before good sense takes over," he countered.

"Not on your life. Take your time."

"Don't you feel overdressed?" he asked in a mocking tone. She flexed the muscles of her abdomen, and her sweat pants fell to the floor. "Not any more. But you sure look stupid standing there with nothing on but your socks." Somehow she had gotten her socks off and was completely naked. They had both stopped thinking about the kitchen.

"Now open the champagne and bring it back to the bedroom. I want you to try out this new air mattress."

They both drank long swallows from the bottle. Sandy took the bottle and poured champagne on Jon. Even though it was cold, it didn't have a dampening effect on his ardor. She went down on him and began licking it off. After a few moments he turned her on her back and filled her with champagne before he went down on her. Sandy came with a loud moan.

"Now, please, please, now."

This time they both moaned together as he thrust in deeply.

A little while later Sandy whispered, "Jon, do you love me?"

"You know I do."

"I accepted an offer from the Yancys to go to Commander's Palace for dinner tonight at eight. Do you still love me?"

"Yes, but probably not as much," He kissed her quickly to let her know he was teasing.

After a lengthy shower together, they dressed to go out. "Since you came in the two-seater, we'll have to meet them there. You remember Mary Yancy teaches school with me, and Gary Yancy is an ENT resident at Charity Hospital . . . they have no children."

"Aren't they the ones who have the two Rotweilers?" Jon wanted to have some topics for conversation that didn't involve sick people.

"Yeah."

The Commander's Palace, in the Garden District only a few blocks from Sandy's, was one of New Orleans' premier restaurants. Jon glanced around the filled dining room, "I love the contrast between the white of the table cloths and napkins and the black tuxedos the waiters wear."

The Yancys were in excellent spirits. They had arrived early, and each had a glass of white wine. "What would you guys like to drink?" Gary asked.

"How about a couple of Bellinis?" laughed Sandy, glancing covertly at Jon.

"So ordered."

"How's the job search going for you guys?" she asked.

"I got a great offer from a group in Boise, Idaho. I really like the group. Most of the docs are younger than forty, and they practice good medicine. The pay ain't half bad either." This time a shared glance passed between the Yancys.

"Mary, what about you? What are your thoughts about Idaho?" Jon asked, sipping on his very girly drink.

"I think it's gonna be awfully cold . . . especially after living in New Orleans."

Gary smiled at Sandy, "I bet I saw a case in the E.R. today that you've never seen in all your years of teaching at a private school. A young black boy, eight or nine, came in because he couldn't hear out of his right ear. The school nurse brought him over because she couldn't get him to hold still enough for her to look in the ear. We papoosed him, and . . . "

"What does papoosing mean?" Sandy interjected.

"Oh, that's rolling a kid up in a sheet, wrapping him up with his arms at his side so that he can't struggle. Anyhow, I looked in his ear, and there was a huge glob of dried ear wax plugging the ear canal. I gently dug it out, and underneath all the wax was a dead roach."

"Oh, Gary, I'm used to this kind of dinner talk, but Sandy and Jon aren't. You're gonna ruin their appetites," admonished Mary.

"Well, I was just telling the story to make the point . . . what are the parents doing? What are they thinking about? Sometimes I wonder if the adults even know whose kid they've got with them."

An awkward silence occurred which only Gary didn't seem to notice. "But hey, at least he got to the E.R. That's better than a lot of my patients. If I could 'habla espanol' maybe then I could take a decent history. So at least in Boise, most of my patients should have English as a first language, right, Mary?"

Jon asked, "Do many of your students speak Spanish at home?" glancing at the two women. "I know in my part of Texas, many of the students are first generation."

"First generation, I'll bet," the doctor scoffed.

"Really, Jon, to be in a private school, even a less expensive one such as ours," Sandy said, "Well, it takes some real money. I have a couple of tutoring students with grandparents in Mexico or Costa Rica, but their dads are Tulane engineering grads, who came for the education and stayed."

Mary looked very relieved when the waiter arrived and took their orders. Looking at his menu, Gary said, "With all these rich sauces, I wonder how much butter they go through in a day?"

"Enough to clog a thousand arteries."

Silence prevailed as the group stuffed itself.

Finally, Gary asked Jon, "Is this just a pleasure trip or are you over here on business?"

Jon laughingly replied, "I'm always on the look-out for firms willing to pay me a retainer, but not too many have business in Richmond, Texas. I bought a practice when Smithers, an older lawyer, took down his shingle. I have a nice variety of clients. I draw up a few wills, probate some, and do a little real estate work. I'm hoping to grow the practice, maybe pick up some corporate accounts, but today, right now, I'm here for Mardi Gras and party time."

Gary retorted, "Don't you have that great chocolate lab Cato? Why don't you talk to the people at Purina? Maybe they'd pay you in dog chow, if they wouldn't give you money."

"Cato would love that."

Fortunately the bread pudding soufflé and coffee arrived, stopping all conversation, once again. They watched spellbound as the waiter broke the top of the soufflé and poured the Grand Marnier sauce in the center.

They all had to waddle out.

When they got back to the T-bird, Sandy asked, "Why did you let me eat so much?"

"To punish you for ordering Bellinis—what a waste of good champagne," he said with a leer. "I can think of much better uses."

Sandy laughed, "I didn't want you to drink too much. I didn't want you to be sleepy. The Yancys are taking the street car, which is good. I don't think Gary needs to be driving."

Later as Jon fell asleep, he thought, *Mardi Gras is pure fantasy. I wonder if a love based on Mardi Gras can exist in the real world?*

They slept in the next morning, both waking up about eleven. Sandy went to the bathroom first, returning in a few minutes. "My morning breath is officially gone. It's your turn . . . but hurry I want a good morning kiss."

Jon hurried. Crawling back into bed, he exclaimed, "Toothpaste, gargle, and mouthwash . . .even deodorant. . . do with me as you would."

And she would . . . they made long love savoring every part of each other's body.

Much later Jon walked into the kitchen and glanced out the

window in the back door. "It's raining. I know they don't call off the parade because of rain, and I can think of better ways to spend the time than getting wet. What you say we skip the parade?"

"Every Saturday afternoon, I make gumbo for Dad. He has a little kitchen in his room at the retirement village, and there's a nice widow lady who lives next door that he likes to share it with. I usually eat with them."

"Sandy, if I'm good or if I was good, and I was, good, wasn't I, could you make enough so that the four of us could eat there together? I'd really like to meet your dad."

"You're too sweet. Of course, I was hoping you'd come with me. Now let's go shower!"

"But I'm not dirty."

"What's that got to do with it?"

As they drove toward the retirement village, Jon asked, "Tell me a little about your dad. *The Reader's Digest* version will be fine."

"Dad was born in Teneha, Texas sixty years ago to Irish Catholic parents . . . his name, Kevin O'Rourke, might have clued you in to that. He was the youngest of eleven. After high school, he went to Le Tourneau University in East Texas. He got a degree in big engine repair. He worked for Stewart and Stevenson for over twenty-five years . . . mainly in diesel engine repair. He made good money. I got some scholarships, but they did fine paying for Sophie Newcomb, and that wasn't cheap."

Jon replied," Yeah, my parents said that they'd help out with Tulane as much as they could. Filling out the financial aid forms and helping me find summer jobs was probably as much as they could." He laughed, "They did more than that, but I have a brother two years older than I am, who went to a state school. He certainly had a lot more spending money based on the same level of help. I'd say that if your dad sent you to college without a whimper, he was doing just fine."

Sandy squeezed his arm and continued, "When Mom found out

she had breast cancer about ten years ago, he retired from Stewart and Stevenson and set up his own facility in Lake Charles. He always thought you got the best care at Catholic hospitals, and the Sister of Charity of the Incarnate Word had a big facility there. He said it always made him feel better seeing the penguins running up and down the halls."

"Penguins?"

"The nuns . . . you know they used to wear those black habits with the white collars. He said it made him think of penguins."

"Also, he got a lot of work on marine diesels. Lake Charles is a pretty good-sized port. When Mother died, it hit him pretty hard, but he kept on working.

"Then about five years ago, he began complaining about back pain. His doctor took X-rays and said he had osteoporosis and arthritis. Heavy duty anti-inflamatories and calcium tablets helped a little bit, but he kept getting worse, and he had to quit work. One day he slammed his car door just like he always had, but this time he fractured his forearm just above his wrist. X-rays showed what the doctors called a 'pathologic fracture.' This meant that something was already wrong with the bone, and a normal action caused the fracture. About this time I got into the act and brought him to the Tulane Medical Center. In about five minutes, the doctors diagnosed far advanced multiple myeloma. He got radiation treatment for his fracture site and chemotherapy for everything else. He did pretty well for a while but he's had several bouts of pneumonia which have weakened him. And he has quite a bit of bone pain."

"I didn't know bones could hurt."

"Jon, Jon, Jon. Have you ever broken a bone? Didn't it hurt? Well, in Daddy's case, lotsa cancer cells have replaced the normal bone cells, and it hurts like a jillion tiny fractures.

"Anyway, I moved him here to New Orleans. He has a nice place in a Catholic run retirement village. He's close, and I get to mother him a bit. I want him to know I'm near, but I don't want to smother him. I was an only child . . . Mother had severe bleeding complications when I was born, and they had to do a hysterectomy.

"I'm afraid you got more of an explanation than you wanted."

"No. That was great. You gave me just the right amount of background. If you were my client being cross-examined, it might have been too much. It must be expensive to keep him housed and for all his medical expenses." Jon was afraid that Sandy would be offended by his probing, but he was worried about her, so he pushed on.

"Well, he had saved a bunch of money through the years. He also did well when he sold his business, but it's getting a little tight these days. We'll figure out something. How do you think I'd do if I set up an escort service in the French Quarter?" she said with a big wink.

"I refuse to dignify that with a response . . . I'd probably have to declare bankruptcy, buying all your time to keep others away. I tease about running a Rent-A-Date agency, but that's just to let you know that you're the only one I care about," Jon was glad she had taken the questioning well, but sorry that he had been right about her financial situation.

"Do they allow your dad to take a drink now and again?"

"With the name Kevin O'Rourke, you ask a question like that?"

"Well, I thought that the village might have rules."

"It's a Catholic run outfit," Sandy said

"So why don't we stop at that liquor store up ahead? Irish whiskey, I presume?" Jon asked while pulling into the little strip center's parking lot.

"You got it."

"Be right back," he said as he hopped out of the car.

Kevin O'Rourke's apartment was on the first floor of a very new, very clean facility. He had a small kitchen, a bedroom-sitting room combination, and a small bath. The carpet was a deep green with a bedspread of green and gold with matching curtains. A couch and two Queen Anne type chairs also done in green and gold filled the sitting area. An old leather recliner had a football pennant draped over the back. The room shouted the influence of Notre Dame. On the wall was a picture of Sandy in a drum major's outfit twirling her baton. A gold-framed picture on the headboard showed a beautiful, redheaded woman, undoubtedly Sandy's mother. Valentines covered the wall, handmade gifts from Sandy's students. Jon recognized Sandy's influence everywhere.

Mr. O'Rourke himself, a large man with a pale complexion, sat in the recliner. He was bald with tufts of reddish and grey hair around the sides of his head. He wore a red flannel shirt and blue jeans. He had on fleece-lined house shoes. When he saw Sandy, his eyes lit up, and a smile filled his face.

"Dad, I want you to meet Jon Miller, the shyster lawyer from Richmond I've told you about."

"Don't much trust lawyers . . . Sandy says you're all right." He extended his hand, and Jon shook it.

"I didn't know she ever said anything nice about me. I am glad to meet you, sir."

"Jon, did you get the shrimp out of the refrigerator like I asked? I don't see them in the stuff I brought in."

"Ouch! I forgot. Have I lost most-favored nation status?"

"Not if I get to take your fancy car and get to go buy some shrimp."

"Here are the keys. Will twenty bucks be enough for the shrimp?"

"Your guilt must be great, offering to pay. I'll be back in a few minutes. I think the Rockets basketball game is on now. Dad's a pretty big fan." She blew him a kiss as she ran out the door. She was right; he did feel guilty about intentionally putting the shrimp back in her refrigerator, but he needed some private time with her dad, and a trip for more shrimp was the best he had been able to come up with. If he had asked directly, Sandy would have been too worried that a 'serious father/boyfriend' talk would upset her dad. And it might, but Jon was going to play it by ear. It might also comfort the older man a lot.

Mr. O'Rourke turned on the T.V. and selected the channel using the remote. Jon said, "I know it's a bit early, but could I interest you in a drop of cheer while we watch the game? Sandy said this brand would be fine," holding up the bottle he had brought.

"I never drink before five P.M., but I'm sure it's after five somewhere. You'll find glasses in the cupboard and ice in the 'fridge.'"

The old man seated himself gingerly in the recliner. A look of pain briefly crossed his face. "Don't be too stingy with that stuff. You know you need a bit to get a good taste of it."

"Yes, sir," said Jon, adding a large extra slug to the other man's glass.

"How do you and Sandy know each other?"

"We met on a blind date when she was at Sophie Newcombe, and I was at Tulane. Best blind date I ever had."

"She asked you to come for Mardi Gras?"

"Yes, sir, just like last year, but I didn't get to meet you then."

They watched the ball game in silence for a few minutes. Then the older man turned to Jon, "You gonna marry her?"

"Sandy said you don't beat around the bush. I want to marry her very much. I've asked her several times . . . all I get back is 'All in due time, Jon. All in due time.' So you tell me, am I?"

"With Sandy, that's as good as 'Yes.' Words of advice from an old man . . . don't rush her. She has a mind of her own. But she'll be well worth the wait for any man she chooses. Good luck. Why don't you freshen my drink a little?"

"I moved to Richmond a few years ago. Bought a practice from a guy name Smithers, who wanted to retire. Do some wills, probate, and a little real estate. I've got one corporate client, Hays Chemical, a hand-me-down from Smithers. So far the practice is doing pretty well. It's growing every year."

"Back when I worked in Lake Charles, I used to do some repair work for Hays. They ran a bunch of tugs up and down the intracoastal canal. Always paid off like gang-busters. Kept their stuff in first-class shape."

Jon had just returned to his seat when Sandy popped in with a bag of shrimp. "Hey, small-town lawyer. How about you chop veggies while I get the rue going?" Jon smiled. This was going really well. He had her father's blessing, and they hadn't had a scene. Yes, he was pretty smooth, if he did say so himself. O.K., so he was only passable with the Yancys the other night, but batting five hundred wasn't bad, not bad at all. Besides the Yancys were moving anyway.

Within minutes the air was filled with the aroma of gumbo. "Is Mrs. Crawford going to come eat with us this evening? I sure do think she's cute."

"Yeah. Me, too. But she's gone to visit her daughter in New Iberia. She said she'll take a rain-check. She says Mardi Gras is the time to get outa town."

After about thirty more minutes, Sandy spoke, "Jon, you're not through. Would you please set the table for three? The utensils are in the second drawer."

Jon dutifully set the table. "Where are the napkins?"

Sandy laughed, "I thought you small town boys used the ends of your sleeves."

"Not when we're with company."

"Well, if you insist on napkins, they're in the far cabinet."

Sandy proved to be as good a cook as she was lovely a woman. After they had eaten and the dishes were washed, Jon said, "I've got something in the car, a *Sports Illustrated*, for your dad. I'll be back in just a minute."

Jon quickly went to the manager's office. "Hi. I'm an old friend of Mr. O'Rourke. He loaned me some money a number of years ago," he lied, "and now won't take anything when I'm trying to pay him back. Would you take this check and apply it to his room and board? I think it ought to cover the next three months. Please don't tell him where it came from."

"This is somewhat irregular, but hey! Money's money. Sure. You want a receipt?"

"Yeah, you might as well. My name's right there on the check."

"O.K., Mr. Miller, here you go and thanks."

Jon got the *Sports Illustrated,* his copy that had come just before he left Richmond and returned to find Sandy helping her dad into the recliner.

"Dad, we're going down to see the parade. Can we get you anything before we leave?"

"Another touch of that Irish Mist might be nice."

They went back to her garage apartment and changed into their costumes. Sandy was Maid Marian and Jon was Robin Hood. They drove to the French Quarter and parked in the garage of the Sheraton Hotel. They walked to Bourbon Street. They went in a building at the corner of Bourbon and Canal, which had a stairway leading to a second story apartment. James Bryant, an old friend of Sandy's, owned the building, which had a balcony overlooking the street, an ideal place to view the parade.

People in all manner of costumes from the sedate to the risqué soon filled the apartment and the sidewalks on both sides of the street. Soon the floats and bands came by . . . the jazz was wonderful. And to make Jon happy, there were a number of women who flashed their bare breasts. Riders on the floats threw hundreds of the cheap necklaces made with plastic beads. Jon took a number of the necklaces and put them over Sandy's head, using them as a lasso to pull her to him for a lingering kiss.

After a while the press of the people became too much for them. Sandy whispered, "Had enough?"

Jon replied, "Enough of this. Some quality time at your place would be nice."

Hand in hand, they walked through the crowded streets, across Canal Street, and to the parking garage. As soon as they were in the car and driving back to the garage apartment, Sandy said, "I need to ask you something. Did you pay the retirement village for Dad's room and board?"

"How did you find out? They agreed not to tell you who paid." Guess that was an admission of guilt.

"The receipt fell on the floor when you changed into your costume. You didn't have to do that."

"I just wanted to help, and I knew you wouldn't take a direct offer. You're not mad at me, are you?"

"Jon, I'll show you how I feel about this just as soon as we get home. Until then just know I think you are the sweetest man I've ever met."

"Hello, Samuel Cox, here."

"Hello, my name is Emma Anderson. I'm calling from Houston, and I'd like to speak to Ann Cox."

"Ann's over at the restaurant. Let me give you that number, and then I'll try to transfer you. Sometimes the transfers get lost. Got something to write with?"

"Yes."

"904-555-1234. Now I'll try the transfer."

"The Quail's Nest. How may I help you?"

"Ann Cox, please."

"Who may I say is calling?"

"Emma Anderson. She probably won't recognize the name."

"Hello, this is Ann. What can I do for you?"

"Hello. My name is Emma Anderson. I'm calling from Houston. I'd like to come out to Leakey to talk to you and your husband about the baby you had recently."

"I'm sorry . . . I don't know who you are or how you got my name, but I don't want to talk about that subject."

"Wait, I'm carrying a baby with the same abnormality. I need to talk to somebody. Please!"

"How did you get my name?"

"I went to work for the doctor in Houston who keeps the national registry, and I stole the list of Texas names. I was desperate."

"Oh, my God! That's different." Ann said, thinking quickly. She didn't want to talk about the baby they had lost, but she could hear the desperation in Emma's voice. "Sure, when do you want to come?"

"Would tomorrow be O.K.? I could leave here in the morning and be in Leakey in the afternoon," Emma suggested hopefully. The sooner that she met with them, the sooner she would have some answers.

"Fine. I'll book you a room in the motel. It's the only one for fifty miles in any direction."

"Thank you. I'll see you tomorrow in the middle of the afternoon."

CHAPTER 6

I t's easy to get to Leakey. Go to San Antonio, get on 90-A west, and turn right on State 127 at Sabinal. It's the first motel on your right . . . about forty-five or fifty miles past your turn," said the lady at Triple A, and she was right. Emma stopped for gas in San Antonio and drove through a Burger King. Now that she was on her quest, and not bothered by morning sickness, fast food seemed like the right approach. She even ordered a large diet Coke—what could it hurt? Not her, not the baby. The whole trip took about five hours, some of which she spent checking her voice mail and talking to Daphne about clients, and generally trying to cover the fact that she was out of the office on a weekday.

Indeed the Leakey Lodge was the first motel either on the right or the left. Made of stone, it looked like something from the fifties. Everything appeared clean. The woodwork was freshly painted; the lawn was clipped and edged. The pool sparkled. A pavilion with tables and chairs was poolside.

Emma entered the office which also served as the entrance to the adjoining café. The place was spotless. A deep green carpet still showed marks of having been recently vacuumed. Emma rang the bell on the desk. Within seconds a slender, nice looking young lady appeared. She had shoulder-length brown hair and large auburn eyes. A pleasant smile crossed her face, "May I help you?"

"My name is Emma Anderson. I have a reservation, and I would like to see Ann Cox."

"Yes, you have a room, and I'm Ann." Ann almost added 'Nice to meet you,' but this was such an odd situation, talking to someone who admitted stealing her personal information.

"I've seen you before. Wait, weren't you Ann Crowley? Weren't you about two years behind me at Lamar High School in Richmond-Rosenberg? I was Emma Coleman before I married Bill Anderson."

"Goodness! It's a small world. Your dad is Dr. Coleman, isn't he? He was our doctor when we were growing up. Here's the key to number nine . . . it's back farthest from the road and the quietest. I turned on the AC earlier to clear out the stale air. Come to the café about six. My husband Samuel will be here, and we can have dinner together and talk. You remember Samuel, don't you? He was five years ahead of me in school. I fell in love with him when I was four and he was nine. I dropped my ice cream cone and he gave me his. I want him with us when we talk."

"Of course, I think that it's better to talk to both of you, if you will."

At six Emma walked to the café. A cool breeze rustled the leaves in the trees around the pavilion. Otherwise it was totally quiet and peaceful.

"Come on in and sit down. You must be Emma. I'm Samuel Cox. I think I was a grade or two ahead of you at Lamar. Ann mentioned that we're all from Lamar CISD, kinda funny, isn't it? I guess I really should say Lamar High School, now that Lamar Consolidated Independent School District has three high schools. Things have really changed in the Richmond area. Anyhow Wednesday night is usually pretty slow so we ought to be able to talk in private."

Ann came out of the kitchen and greeted them both. "Emma, your choice of nights was great. Wednesday is slow so I can leave the restaurant work to David and Mary, and I can play customer here, or we can go to the pizza place or the Mexican restaurant." Ann was nervous about the upcoming conversation and caught herself chattering.

"I'm fine here, as long as you will let me buy the dinner. I know you own the place, but it's still nice of you to let me come and to talk to me." Emma wasn't completely used to having to convince witnesses, since usually the witnesses worked for her client and were very eager to help her, but she could be convincing if she had to be.

They sat down at a table by the window looking out on the

highway. A heavy, matronly woman came out and took their order. After Mary left, Emma spoke first, "How in the world did you end up out here?"

Ann replied, "Samuel and I had dated forever. When he graduated from college and entered law school, I had just graduated from high school. We married and lived in Houston. I waited tables and managed a small restaurant which was excellent training for what I do now. Samuel worked for a firm in Houston, and we bought a small house in the 'burbs. We had both grown up in the country . . . actually Thompsons and really were not all that happy in a huge place like Houston. By then we had two kids, and the thought of public schools in Houston was frightening. So when my uncle died and left us this lodge, we moved."

Samuel reached into his wallet and pulled out pictures. "The boy is Justin . . . he's three and Marla's four." Parental pride filled Samuel and Ann's faces. "The kids eat at their aunt's house on Wednesday and usually sleep over. Fortunately that's where they were when we had our night of terror."

Emma looked puzzled. "Oh, forgive me. That's what we call the night I had the baby. Let's start at the beginning since that is what you came all this way to talk about." Ann paused, and Samuel took up the story.

"We'd been quite concerned about medical care here in Leakey. There's a retired G.P. who visits once a month. The nearest hospital of any size is in Kerrville, about two hours away. I was very worried. I am the fourth of five children. My mother had major complications at the birth of my brother, the one just older than me. The doctor didn't recognize the problems, and they didn't do a C-section in time. He had major brain damage and has been institutionalized since birth." This time Samuel paused, and Ann picked up.

"That's when Samuel's mother started going to your dad. Your dad had quite a reputation among the women of Thompsons and Richmond for his sympathetic and caring treatment. He delivered both Samuel and me."

"My dad had a great reputation with me, too. I was devastated when he died. I was a junior at Rice. I'm really sorry that he didn't get to see me married and in a law practice. So many people in Richmond were so supportive. Did you know that we established a foundation, the Jess Coleman foundation? It's not at all comparable to the Albert foundation, but the Jess Coleman foundation concentrates on education enhancements to benefit the Lamar CISD. Daddy had a very extensive stamp collection, and I gave that to the library as the cornerstone of a collection. My board of directors keeps looking for ways to continue his commitment to the community," Emma concluded. "It's still a long way from Richmond to Leakey, so please continue."

"Any way we figured that we were both young and in good health. If I got pregnant again, it would be our third, and I hadn't had any complications with the other deliveries so we thought 'what the heck.'

"We moved out here and re-did the lodge. We did most of the work ourselves. We lived in the apartment above the office for a month or two. Then a house on the square across from the courthouse came available, and we moved there. Somehow in the move, a certain article . . . a diaphragm . . . got misplaced, and I got pregnant. Not planned, but not unwanted." Ann blushed slightly and looked at Samuel.

"I had just seen the G.P. out here . . . it was my seventh month. I know I should have seen somebody earlier. But I didn't. I was scheduled to see an O.B. in Kerrville the next week. The night I miscarried, a 'blue norther' had blown in. The roads were covered with ice and snow. My goodness what a trip. I was cold, scared, and having contractions. Samuel got us to Kerrville somehow. The doctor I had the appointment with met us at the hospital and took care of me. He's a real jewel. He said that he wasn't any good at emotional counseling, but he talked to me for about thirty minutes while Samuel was eating breakfast the next morning. I've never met a kinder, more understanding man. Anyway the baby was severely deformed. The area over the spine and skull hadn't fused. It was awful. They didn't want me to see the baby, but I had to. Samuel and I saw the baby the morning after he was born. On the front, he just looked very premature, but on the back . . ." Tears ran down Ann's face. Samuel gently put his hand over hers. Emma noticed the comforting gesture, and looked at the couple. They were a unit. It was their grief, not just Ann's, and they were comforting, supporting each other. She didn't know why she was surprised, but she was.

"They sent the baby to the medical school in San Antonio," Samuel continued softly. "They did an autopsy and DNA analysis. They came and got specimen from each of us. They said that we both had a defect in the thirteenth chromosome. They said that statistically one out of four of our children would be affected since it was a recessive trait." Emma nodded. She had heard this before.

Ann continued, "They strongly advised us not to have any more children so Samuel got a vasectomy. We had the children checked. Mary was normal. Justin was found to be a carrier, just like us. We'll tell him when he's older. We'll tell him to have his wife tested before they try to have kids. For now, they just know that their brother is in heaven."

Samuel finished the story. "Our family lost a number of children at childbirth in preceding generations. It's a family tradition; we don't name the child that dies at birth. He's always just Baby Boy Cox. That's what's on his tombstone. But he's a member of our family.

"Now tell us your story," Samuel said, as their order arrived.

"You know that I married Bill Anderson while we were in college. After we got out of UT law school, Bill and I tried to get pregnant for two years before going to a fertility expert. I'm in the tax group at the Houston law firm." Samuel registered some surprise at the firm, then more surprise as Emma told them where Bill practiced.

"A couple of months after we saw Dr. Wornat, I got pregnant. At my first visit, he did an ultrasound and was worried. I had an MRI that confirmed that my baby has rachischisis, the failure of the spine to close from the same defect on the thirteenth chromosome. The doctor recommended terminating the pregnancy, but," Emma's voice broke and she looked away from the table. Everyone else busied themselves with their meal.

"So you've had pretty high powered care all along, and that didn't help," Ann said. "I don't know that this will help you, but it's comforting to me to understand that knowing earlier wouldn't have helped."

"It doesn't help. I haven't had an abortion," Emma said. "I can't. But I want some answers. I have to find out why. I want to know who is to blame. I want to know how Bill and I ended up with this defect. That's why I went to work in the geneticist's lab. That's how I got your name." Samuel noticed that Emma covered herself enough that he would not be obligated to report her theft and misbehavior to the State Bar.

"The doctors have told me that they don't know what the cause is. They suggested that genetic mutations could be caused by irradiation or exposure to toxic chemicals. Were either of you exposed? With the four of us being from the same area, exposure to something in the Rosenberg-Richmond area when we were growing up would sure have to be considered."

Samuel answered, "The doctors from San Antonio asked us the same questions, over and over again. Neither Ann nor I knew of any exposure. We had been healthy all our lives."

Mary emerged from the kitchen with three of the largest portions of bread pudding Emma had ever seen. When the empties were cleared, attention turned to steaming cups of coffee which finished the meal.

After the table was cleared, Ann turned to Emma, "Why have you continued this pregnancy? Knowing the outcome, I'm not sure I could do that. That's why Samuel had the vasectomy and I made sure he had the test to say that it worked. I couldn't do that again. Emma, whatever you do, don't look at the baby."

"I am Catholic . . . I can't terminate a pregnancy if the baby is still alive."

"Talk to your priest. Surely something can be done. I think that the longer you go, the worse it gets. I'm sorry," Ann's sympathy was sincere, Emma realized. And it might be the first sympathy without strings that she had received.

"Where's your husband Bill?" Samuel asked, and Emma knew his courtroom instincts were kicking in.

She'd have to be careful how she answered, "He's in Houston. His caseload is pretty heavy. He's in the contracts section, so it's pretty intense when there's a new contract negotiation going on, like now. I was fine on the drive out."

"I guess I meant, where is he on your search for answers?" Samuel prodded.

"He wants to know what caused it, too, but honestly, he wants to try again. You remember his dad coached baseball, and Bill played baseball at Rice. He loves sports. He wants healthy sons to play baseball with." Emma's voiced dropped at the admission.

Suddenly Samuel got a very strange look on his face. "Do you remember when all the cattle died?"

"What are you talking about?" Emma asked. "What cows?"

"Well," said Samuel, "My dad was manager of that little private chemical plant down near Thompsons. Let's see, Zunker Chemical was the name of the company. During the Viet Nam war, they made some kind of chemicals down there for the army. Dad never could say what it was they made . . . top secret stuff . . . but there were rumors that it was a nerve gas made from crude oil that they got directly from the Thompsons field. Anyhow they had some sort of a 'spill.' All the cattle in the surrounding fields died. That was about the time that Hays Chemical bought the place. They brought in the EPA and everything was 'taken care of.' I wonder . . ."

"When was this?"

"I was in the fourth grade, I remember. I had just started playing little league baseball. The company sponsored a league. That's why I remember. The field next to the park had some cows that died, and we saw them at practice."

"Who can tell me more about this? Is your dad still alive?" Emma spit out the questions rapidly, happy to have her first real lead.

"Dad and Mom are both dead. I think most of the people who worked in that plant have died, not from any specific cause but just because it was a long time ago. You'd have to check with Hays to see who worked there."

Emma was too wired to sleep. She started back to Houston the next morning after a brief and tearful good-by to Ann and Samuel.

During the drive back, she kept remembering the closeness that Ann and Samuel shared. They were so loving. *How do Bill and I look?* Emma wondered. *I think we're more of a partnership with separate roles. The Coxes seemed like a set, a unit. They looked like they really belong together, a matched set.*

Emma made plans to find out more about the plant and the people who had worked there. It was too soon to cut off any avenues to pursue, but she had a good feeling about this. With the chemical spill, she was sure she was finally on the track to get some answers. Unlike Bill had suggested, this was far from a wasted trip, well worth the weekend she was going to give to make up the hours. She always got more done when she was in her office by herself, anyway, she rationalized.

"My name is Emma Anderson, and I'm calling to see if I can come to talk to you about your recent pregnancy." There was a loud clunk followed by a dial tone.

Emma re-dialed the Dallas number of Rachel Davis. As soon as there was a pick-up, she said, "Please don't hang up until you hear what I have to say. I'm carrying a baby diagnosed with the same abnormality that affected your pregnancy. I have to talk to someone. I obtained your name and number from the office of the doctor who has the national registry. Please let me come and talk to you!"

"I'll talk to you, but there are conditions. One: my husband must know nothing of this. Two: I will only meet with you in a public place. Three: there will be only one meeting."

"Agreed."

"We will meet in the lobby of the Adolphus Hotel in downtown Dallas. Do you know where it is?"

"Yes."

"I will be in the lobby with the registration desks at noon on Thursday. I will wear a blue blouse with a blue and red scarf. There will be no second chance if you are late. Don't call me back."

Emma heard a soft click and then the sound of a dial tone.

Emma took "The Company Plane," as Southwest Airlines advertising wanted you to call it, leaving Hobby Field in Houston at nine Thursday morning. She walked out the front door of Dallas Love Field a little after ten and caught the first cab in line. Within fifteen minutes, she alighted in front of the Adolphus Hotel, one of the great old hotels in Dallas. She quickly found the registration lobby and sat in a cushioned chair across from the registration desk. At exactly twelve noon, a good-looking woman in her mid-thirties came in the front entrance. She wore a blue blouse and a blue and red scarf tied about her neck. She was tall, fashionably thin, and a brunette by the grace of Miss Clairol.

Emma Anderson advanced toward her, "Mrs. Davis, Mrs. Rachel Davis?"

"Yes."

"I'm Emma Anderson. Thank you very much for coming."

"Let's talk over lunch in the hotel coffee shop. It's usually very quiet in there."

Rachel led the way to the coffee shop and sat in a far corner. After they ordered, Emma broke the silence, "I am still pregnant with a baby that has the same diagnosis that caused you to terminate your pregnancy. I am a devout Catholic and termination of a pregnancy would cause me a great deal of grief. My marriage is already shaky, and I think that this may destroy it. Can you talk to me about your situation?" On the flight up she had planned her strategy and had settled on the woman-to-woman approach.

"I recognize you," Rachel exclaimed. "You used to be Emma Coleman. Your dad was the town doctor. My mom and dad both went to him. Do you still drive Corvettes?"

"Afraid not. Strictly sedans now. What was your maiden name?"

"I was Rachel Stibora. I was a couple of years ahead of you at Lamar High School. I was a blond in those days."

"I remember you now. Didn't you live on Timber Lawn in Rosenberg? Your dad had a beer distributorship."

"Right you are.

"You wanted my story. Here is the abridged version.

"I married Brad Davis after my second year at U.T. after he knocked me up. He had just finished getting his Masters in petroleum engineering. We have two children . . . the first, a girl and two years later, a boy. Both are great kids. Brad has done very well. We've been able to move into University Park. I went back to college and got a degree in English. I now work as a volunteer and soccer mom. I'm trying to keep from losing my position as an executive wife to a new trophy wife." She sounded more resigned than sad.

"I convinced my husband to have a vasectomy because the pill made me gain weight, the diaphragm was messy, and an IUD caused severe menstrual cramping. The jerk used the vasectomy as a means to let him screw his secretary. I used my high school class reunion as a one-night stand. You may even remember the guy . . . Ernie Schulze. He was the world's biggest geek," she was recounting the facts in a flat voice, but her tone warmed at the mention of Ernie's name.

"I remember him well. So Ernie, also born in Richmond, was the father?" Emma was focused on the facts that would support her claim against the chemical company.

"Yeah, your father may have delivered him. I know he delivered me.

"Anyway, I had an abortion early on. I would have had one anyway because I think I still love Brad. I'm Baptist, so it wasn't an easy choice. Maybe knowing the baby wouldn't have lived makes it better. Anyway, my doctor sent the fetus to Southwestern Medical School. He told me that there were abnormalities on the thirteenth chromosome. He said that I may be a carrier, and I should be tested. He said it may be a good idea to have the kids tested. I told him I'd tell the kids to be tested when they got older and could understand. I think I meant when I can work out an explanation about how I know I have this," she said honestly.

Emma asked, "Have you ever been exposed to any toxic chemicals or irradiation?"

"Nothing except Ernie's toxic semen," she answered sadly. The animation she had shown earlier was gone. She was back to resigned and a little sad.

"Do you know anything about a plant that was down in Thompsons during the Viet Nam War?" Emma wanted to be thorough with her questions.

"Rumors said they made nerve gas but nobody really knew. Why?" she didn't show much interest.

"Just wondering. Thank you so much for meeting with me; it's helped. I won't bother you any more."

Emma flew back to Houston on the three o'clock plane.

CHAPTER 7

At about five months, in the middle of March, Emma began to show. She requested and received a medical leave of absence from her law firm. She wrapped up all her pending active cases. Other than Daphne, she only explained the true situation to her section chief, a man with three children and several grandchildren. He was very sympathetic as Emma had been sure he would be. She had positioned the pregnancy as something she and Bill had both wanted, using her pregnancy just like she used every other asset or advantage that she had. She expected the pregnancy to be fewer than forty weeks, something that Wornat had told her when trying yet again to talk her into having an abortion. She wouldn't need the full amount of leave time because she wouldn't be making arrangements for child care, but her section chief didn't need to know that. She rationalized it by reminding herself that most new mothers don't use all that time for the baby—that's just what the system gives you. She knew she was entitled to that much time, and she would take as much time as she wanted.

Bill had moved out of the house about three weeks earlier. The bitter quarrels over termination of the pregnancy had proved too much for Bill. During one of the fights that had started out as a discussion of adoption, he had tried to explain to her that he wanted to teach his son to throw a baseball. He wanted to pass on his skill to someone who had the same physical obstacles to overcome or to learn to compensate for as he had had growing up. Bill said he wanted a son who was part of himself or a daughter who had his athletic abilities and Emma's phenomenal intellect, trying to spark a similar desire in his wife. He said, "That's why I want to keep trying to have a son or daughter of our own." What she heard was "If you can't give me a son, I'll find someone who can."

When she replied, "Fine, Bill, go find someone else to knock up," he was too stunned and hurt to say anything. When he thought about it, he decided they needed some breathing room; he hadn't given up on getting Emma to try again. He was regrouping. He was sure she'd come around, and giving her some space would help.

Her appointments with Dr. Wornat increasingly turned into shouting matches about ending the pregnancy. At six months, Emma's ankles began to swell badly. Dr. Wornat put her on salt restriction and a diuretic. It helped a little. Her depression and anger grew.

Emma hated her doctor, who acted like a trail boss who wanted to "thin the herd" and destroy any evidence that any one of his patients might have had a bad outcome. She hated her religion and the male Pope who decreed what a woman could do with her body. He would never be pregnant and couldn't really understand. She hated Bill who had no feeling for her and who only wanted a son. Mainly she hated herself for getting into a situation where she was not in control and where she would lose. Without the images of her mother's self-destruction, Emma would have started drinking.

At seven months, Emma went to Dr. Wornat's office for her monthly appointment. She was weighed, her blood pressure was taken, and samples of urine and blood were obtained. She was then escorted back to Dr. Wornat's personal office. She sat in one of the high-backed leather chairs waiting. She heard people entering the room and the door closing. She turned and saw Dr. Wornat, Bill, and Father Fleming, her parish priest. "What the Hell is going on here?" she demanded to know.

Dr. Wornat spoke, more softly and gently than she had ever heard him, "Emma, you have edema in both legs, your blood pressure is elevated, and you have protein in your urine. This is a condition known as pre-eclampsia. It can lead to eclampsia with convulsions and even death. The only sure cure for this is to deliver the fetus. I had Bill bring your priest here to discuss this with you, to give the church's perspective. I know that you and your husband have separated, but I felt he had a right to be part of the discussion."

"Emma," said Father Fleming with love in his voice, "Your God loves you as one of his own. The church does not expect you to carry this child at the expense of your own life. Deliver the child, now, please."

Bill whispered, "Emma, I still love you. We can make it together. Give up the pregnancy."

Rage welled up with in her throat, and she wanted to scream, but instead she started to cry. Bill bent down and began to stroke her shoulders. Lifting her head and wiping her eyes, Emma yielded, "When can we schedule this, and what do we do?"

"Nancy will schedule you at the hospital in the morning. Don't eat or drink anything after ten tonight. We'll start an I.V. and infuse Pitocin. This will induce labor. I expect you to have a normal vaginal delivery. If the fetus is born alive, we will support it. I do not think it will live long, if at all. You can go home the following morning."

"Bill, would you take me home? I need someone with me."

"Sure. Father and I drove over here together in his car. I'll pick mine up later at the church."

At the front desk, Nancy said, "Be at Labor and Delivery at the hospital at seven in the morning. Don't eat or drink anything after ten this evening."

Nancy didn't say anything else, but Emma got out her checkbook to pay.

The next morning Bill and Emma arrived about fifteen minutes early. Bill had stayed the night and had been very sympathetic. Emma wasn't sure if this would be a permanent arrangement. Surprisingly Labor and Delivery was easily found; signs clearly marked the way. One presumes that they didn't want a woman in labor to get lost and deliver in the hall. Again surprisingly all the paper work had been done by Dr. Wornat's office. Even the insurance had been arranged.

A cute, young candy-striper led Bill to the waiting area. A

nurse took Emma to a labor room. Emma changed into a hospital gown. Putting her clothes in a duffel bag provided, Emma gave it to the nurse. Emma had made sure not to wear any jewelry, not even her wedding ring or her carat and a half engagement ring.

After about five minutes, a young man in green scrubs came into the room. "I'm Dr. Ford, an anesthesiologist on the staff here. I will do a very brief physical exam. Dr. Wornat has already provided a detailed history and physical. Do you have any allergies?"

"Not that I know of."

He listened to her heart and lungs, noted her swollen ankles, and poked gently on her abdomen. "We want to make this as pain free as possible. We will start an I.V. with dextrose in water running in very slowly . . . this is to keep access open to your veins so that we can give you any necessary medicine without having to stick you again. For pain we can use an epidural anesthesia. We put a small plastic tube into the spinal canal and inject an anesthetic."

"I had a spinal anesthesia when I had my appendix removed."

"Well, it's not exactly the same . . . but close. If you're not having much discomfort we might be able to manage things with I.V. morphine. In any event, I need you to sign a permit allowing me to do this and a permit for Dr. Wornat to do the delivery. Any questions?"

Emma scrawled her name at the bottom of the two sheets.

"Now we'll add some Pitocin to the I.V. to induce your labor. Your husband can come back and visit if you want."

"Send him on back." Lying there alone for a moment, Emma mused on her situation. . . . *This is no fun . . . I'm not sure Bill is worth it. I won't do this again . . . rachichisis or no rachichisis. It might be worth it if I'd get something to bring home with me from the hospital . . . Bill can just accept the fact that any kid in our marriage is going to be adopted.*

After about thirty minutes Emma began noticing an occasional contraction. After the third or fourth contraction, a short, red-headed young nurse in blue scrubs breezed into the room. "Could you excuse us for a few minutes, Mr. Anderson? I'm Wendy Morris, a Labor and

Delivery RN. We need to take care of a few housekeeping chores, like bedpans, catheters, checking progress, and washing things up. You can come back in about fifteen minutes. There's a little snack bar just down the outer hall. The coffee's good, and the sticky buns are to die for. I'll holler at you when you can come back." With that she ushered him out.

"Housekeeping" took only about ten minutes. Wendy said, "I'll go get your husband. I'll be back to check on your progress in about twenty or thirty minutes." With that she breezed out. Bill returned looking like he had gotten his caffeine and sugar fix. Emma wanted some caffeine, too, but she knew she would just have to wait.

The contractions became more frequent and stronger. At about two hours, Emma became very uncomfortable. She began to tell Bill just how bad she felt, when Wendy came in to check her progress. She had brought in a hypodermic syringe. She said, "Let's see if some of this 'joy juice' will help your disposition." With that she injected the morphine into the I.V. line. Suddenly Emma may still have been hurting but she just didn't care.

Thirty minutes later they moved Emma onto a stretcher. "We're off to see the Wizard," Wendy announced. To Bill she said, "We're going to the delivery room, Mr. Anderson. Dr. Wornat said that you may come into delivery if you wish. You'll have to change into scrubs."

A frown crossed Bill's face. "I don't handle stuff like this very well. I'll stay in the waiting room."

"Sissy!" hissed Wendy jokingly, and she wheeled Emma down the hall. Fortunately Emma remained in the 'don't care' mood or she would have insisted that Bill accompany her.

In the delivery room Emma saw Dr. Wornat dressed in blue scrubs. He looked funny with the blue cap on his head. They moved Emma to the delivery table and placed her feet in the stirrups. Then they placed sterile drapes over her. They increased the rate of the I.V. slightly. Contractions were coming about every minute. Another jolt of Wendy's 'joy juice,' and Emma didn't care what they did to her.

And then it happened: a monster contraction, a gush of liquid, and a flurry of activity at the lower end of the table. "Emma, it's exactly as we thought. There is a complete lack of fusion. It only breathed twice. I'm sorry."

"I want to see it."

"I don't think it wise," said Dr. Wornat.

The 'don't care' attitude vanished. Emma spoke in a most forceful tone, "I want to see it now." She took one look, and she said, "Take it away. Someone will pay for this."

"Emma," said Dr. Wornat, "You can tell Bill it was a boy." With that he injected something into the I.V., and Emma passed out.

When Emma awoke, it had gotten dark outside, and she had been moved to a private hospital room. Bill and Dr. Wornat were speaking quietly. Seeing Emma's eyes open, Dr. Wornat spoke to her, "You are doing fine and can go home in the morning. We've contacted Father Fleming and the funeral home. You and Bill need to talk in coming days. Statistically there is only a one in four probability of your having another abnormal pregnancy. You may want to try again. You may not. I'll let you rest now."

CHAPTER 8

She had slept most of the first couple of days after getting out of the hospital. Yesterday she and Bill had talked about the services for the baby. Actually she had talked, and he had agreed. Seeing his discomfort and his eagerness to get the funeral done, Emma considered making absurd suggestions, just to see how far she could push him like suggesting a choir at the graveside. But she didn't; Bill didn't intend anything mean by his agreeable approach. In fact, he had treated her with kindness and great concern. He didn't know what to do, so he had lapsed into doing whatever she wanted. Emma could handle that.

She had roused herself, gotten a shower, and begun making the arrangements. She contacted a funeral home, scheduled a limo to take them to the graveside services. She had even chosen a gravesite on some land she owned in Fort Bend County. Now she just had to get through the service.

She had called Angela to tell her. When she had first told her, she had tried to explain that the baby wouldn't live, but Angela had responded with more prayers and more candles. After the delivery Emma had dreaded calling her surrogate mother, but the call had gone better than expected. Angela had cried, but her concern had been for Emma and how she felt. Angela had taken Bill's approach. When she heard about the arrangements she said, "Whatever you want. Whatever you think is best."

The phone rang twice before Emma rolled over and picked it up. She looked at the clock . . . nine fifteen. Bill had left without waking her. "Yeah?" she muttered, stifling a yawn.

"Emma, this is Daphne. Are you ever planning on coming back

to work? They left me in your office for a month fastening down the loose ends. Now I'm back in the pool, and I don't like it."

Daphne was Emma's legal secretary and the closest she had to a true friend. She was a very intelligent, black woman, a single mother of two. Daphne took no prisoners when it came to defending Emma. Daphne was too hard-working and capable to be in the secretarial pool.

Emma snapped awake. Daphne was her major asset at the firm. Sure, Emma knew that she was on partner track. She kept her clients happy and did good work for them, and billed plenty of hours. But she also knew that when she made partner she would owe a lot to Daphne. Keeping Daphne happy worked to her advantage. And Emma knew that other associates on their way to partner would be only too eager to grab a treasure like Daphne out of the pool. She needed to prevent any poaching during her leave.

"I haven't figured what I'm gonna do. I've got to get my personal shit together. You know we're going to have the funeral for our baby. He only lived a few minutes. I really didn't get to bond with him. I've got to figure out what caused all this."

"When's the funeral? I'll be there." Daphne hadn't seen Emma as the perfect mother, but burying a baby had to be hard on anyone. Everyone needed support.

"It's tomorrow. Come by our house about nine thirty. I've got a limousine taking Father Fleming, Bill, and me out to the burial site. My dad had some property down on the Brazos River outside Richmond. We're going to bury the baby on a bluff overlooking the river. Father Fleming will do a short grave-side service. Then we'll probably have lunch before we take Father back to the rectory." Daphne could hear the resignation in Emma's voice. She knew Emma needed to get up and get going on something.

The hard driving rain of the night before had turned into a pervasive drizzle. It was hot, and steam rose from the asphalt streets. The sky was battleship gray with no promise of a break.

Daphne arrived at Emma's house promptly at nine-thirty dressed in a simple navy suit. Emma, Bill, and Daphne sat around the breakfast room table in virtual silence, drinking coffee and eating kolaches. The limousine arrived at ten; Father Fleming was inside seated next to the driver. After perfunctory "good mornings," they rode to the burial site in silence, Bill in a dark suit behind the driver, Daphne in her plain blue suit at the other door, with Emma in a navy blue maternity dress between them.

They drove down the Southwest Freeway through Sugar Land and turned south on State 762. Going north would have taken them to Richmond. Going south from this exit led through the Brazos River bottoms to Thompsons where oil was first discovered in the area. Many of the large farms had been purchased by developers, and rich Houston had spilled over into large country homes. Emma's family had never sold any land, partly because they didn't need the money and partly because they were never sure that Emma's mother would be sober enough to sign the papers. She hadn't set up a guardianship for her mother—no need to. Her mother never went anywhere, Angela sorted the mail before she saw it, and Emma paid all the bills.

Just before reaching Thompsons, Father Fleming turned to the Andersons, "Have you given thought to what name this child should have? I'd like to use it in my prayers."

Emma replied, "We always thought we'd name our first boy after Bill . . . he'd be junior."

"But I didn't want to waste my name or my father's name on something that was going to die at birth," muttered Bill.

"We told the people at the hospital we had chosen to name the baby after my father, David Jesse Coleman. So you can use the name 'David Jesse' in your prayers," said Emma softly. Daphne placed her hand over Emma's. She didn't know everything that was going on, but she knew there wasn't a lot of love in this car.

They drove off the asphalt two-lane farm-to-market road onto a gravel road, which led to Emma's property. They looked ahead and saw the hearse had already arrived. The burial was on a high bluff overlooking the Brazos. Many of Emma's ancestors had chosen this spot for their final resting place because of the beauty and the quiet. A tent with four chairs was set up next to a newly opened grave. A green colored rug floored the tent. The casket, infant-sized and made of a beautiful blue metal, sat on the supports over the tiny grave. *My father is gone. Now, my baby is gone too. Eventually I'll have to find a place to bury my mother—then I won't ever have to come back here,* she told herself.

They were just getting out of the limousine when a large black Cadillac drove up. Angela was driving. Bill exploded, "What the Hell is she doing here?"

Angela and Emma's mother emerged from the Cadillac. Angela ran to Emma's side, "I'm sorry. I told her about the baby. She had to come. She has had nothing to drink this morning except coffee. I want to be here for you, too, and I can't leave her."

"It'll be fine," Emma whispered to Angela and to Bill. "Mother, good morning." Mrs. Coleman nodded to Emma, but Emma wasn't sure she knew who Emma was.

Two additional chairs suddenly appeared, and they all took their places. Angela looked surprised at the small attendance, but quickly focused on the priest as he began to speak.

Father Fleming spoke and prayed briefly. Neither Emma nor Bill listened to a word he said. When the name David Jesse was first spoken in the prayer, Emma's mother uttered a mournful wail and slumped down in her chair. Angela quickly put her arm around Emma's mother to comfort her. They returned to the limousine without waiting for the grave to be filled. Angela and Emma's mother pulled out ahead of them. As they were leaving Thompsons, Emma called to the driver, "Take that oyster-shell road over the tracks."

"Ma'am, I'm not sure this limo can make it over the tracks," the driver looked doubtfully at the grade crossing and path through the field.

"Give it a try," Emma encouraged him. Bill glanced at her somewhat suspiciously, but he didn't speak.

They eased over the tracks barely scraping bottom. About half a mile down the road, they came to a fence blocking the road. The sign read, "Posted. No Admittance. Hays Chemical Company." Emma wrote down the number appearing at the bottom of the sign. In the distance they could see a metallic building. Weeds had grown up through the asphalt parking lot.

Emma slipped the paper with the number into her purse and said, "O.K., we can go now." And then she whispered under her breath, "I'll get them. I'll get the bastards who killed my son."

As the limo started back up the freeway toward Houston, Daphne broke the silence by remarking, "I'm sorry no one else was there."

Emma looked over at her a little surprised. "I didn't tell anyone else. As you probably figured out, I hadn't intended for my mother to be there." Bill made a slight sound of disgust. Emma ignored him and continued, "Who would I tell? Why would I want anyone else there?"

Daphne was dumbfounded that anyone could have so few friends. How could Emma not have people who would rally around her and support her? Daphne thought of all the times she had gone to her friends and her mother's friends when they had a loss. Where were Bill and Emma's friends? The silence lasted until they were back in West U.

As Daphne was getting into her car to go, Emma said to her, keeping her voice low so that no one else heard, "I still have nine months leave I can use before I have to return to work. If I can arrange it with the firm and we can fix it so you don't lose seniority or benefits, would you work for me? I want to get the 'Mothers' who caused all this." Bill had gone into the house after tipping the driver and making sure that Father Fleming would get home or to the church. There wasn't anyone else around, but Daphne was starting to understand Emma's need for privacy.

"Sure. Just let me know when it's set. I'm not doing anything important in the pool." Daphne smiled to herself—this was more like the Emma she knew.

"I'll call you early next week, probably Monday. We'll work here at first and see if I need an office. I'm going to get to the bottom of this. What I've learned is that exposure to certain chemicals can cause the mutation that Bill and I have. We both lived in Richmond and could have been exposed to what Zunker Chemicals made for the government. Now, all I've got to figure out is what they made and how to prove that it caused the mutation. I'm going to get to the bottom of this."

Daphne replied, "Go, girl. Let's get the bastards."

The following Monday Emma phoned Daphne, "I got it approved. You can work for me. The firm will still pay you, and I'll reimburse the firm. Doesn't change the status of your 401k or any of your benefits." For Emma, working it so that Daphne worked for her, got out of the secretarial pool, and kept out of the clutches of all the other partner-track associates justified any amount of rule stretching and policy re-interpretation. That's what tax attorneys did, move the boundaries for their clients. And she represented herself at least as well as she represented anyone else.

401K, sure, Daphne thought, *as if I have money for that. I'll fund 529 education savings accounts for each boy first.* But she recognized that Emma was telling her the details that Emma would want to know.

"Man, that's all right," whooped Daphne.

"Before you leave downtown to come to my house, write a letter to the EPA. Tell them we saw some suspicious barrels down at the old Hays Chemical Plant. Let's see if we can't stir up some trouble. Don't sign it or put my name on it. But do use firm stationery. Here's the 'Report a Rat' address that I got off our last water bill. It says to notify them of any suspected EPA violations." She gave Daphne the information.

"I'll do it. I'll come to your house tomorrow morning. Should I plan on shifting my hours to nine 'til six?"

"No, we're going to do this right. I'll see you at eight tomorrow at my house." Emma felt the stirring of enthusiasm that she associated with the beginning of cases and the day before a courtroom appearance. Yes, she was back on her game. She still had many things to work out, but she had a plan, and she would succeed. She always did.

A few blocks away in the medical center, others were wrapping up another aspect of the Anderson case. "Dr. Wornat, this is Ellen Sims of the Medical Records Office here at the hospital. I'm calling to remind you to finish your charts by Friday. You remember you have the death certificate for the Anderson baby?"

"Yes, yes. I'll come over at noon today. I certainly don't want to be suspended over that case. You know this all could have been avoided if the bitch had agreed to the damn abortion like she should have done." His disgust over the whole situation came through clearly. He caught himself, no need for anyone else to know about the mess. "Thank you. I'll be by at noon. Please make sure the papers are in my box." He hung up with a sigh.

CHAPTER 9

At the beginning of their second week working together at her house, Emma came into the office she had made from one of the guest bedrooms. Daphne was already at the table working, papers spread out everywhere. "Daphne, I'm gonna run these papers out to the Albert Foundation for Mr. Benson's signature. I'm trying to keep up with at least one of my clients. I thought I'd stop by and see Mom. Last time she thought I was her sister but hey! You do what you gotta do. Do you have enough to keep you busy or should I make up some work for you?"

Daphne scowled, "Sister, I've got enough crap to get done to take 'til the Fourth of July. But say 'Hey' to Angela for me. Wish you weren't so busy and weren't so fast. Then I could spread my work out a little." *Emma was coming around*, she thought. Daphne never saw any signs of Bill, but Emma had more energy and plenty of drive. Daphne would give her time and keep working on whatever tasks came her way. Emma had plenty of money to pay her, so it would all work out.

Emma drove to Richmond, the home of the Albert Foundation, the sixth largest philanthropic trust in Texas, set up to benefit the citizens of Fort Bend County, Texas. It was set up by Mr. and Mrs. George Albert, wealthy residents of the county, who died without heirs. Through skillful management and a lot of oil, it had accumulated and distributed a great deal of wealth. The Foundation's tax and non-profit filings were the one responsibility she had kept at the firm during her leave. There weren't heavy tasks, and she knew the director personally, so it had seemed like a good idea. She didn't want someone else getting in front of her on the partner track. The

Albert Foundation combined a high profile with low maintenance making it the perfect client to keep.

The offices of the foundation were housed in an unpretentious one-story building in downtown Richmond. A parking place opened up right in front, and Emma turned in.

"Hello, Emma! What brings you to the dark domain?" shouted Liz, Mr. Benson's secretary and Girl Friday.

"We've got to keep you people tax free, and the evil empire has dreamed up ways to claim some of your money. So like the Fram filter man says, 'You can pay me now or pay Uncle later.' Is the Big Man in?"

"Head right on in. He always says you're too expensive to keep waiting. He says that an idling engine uses gas but doesn't get anywhere."

Emma went into the plain office of Robert Benson, head of the Foundation. A roll-top desk, a couch, a couple of chairs, and two filing cabinets made up the furniture. The floor was a dark brown Mexican tile. Benson was a balding, middle-aged man who had spent his life guarding the Foundation money. His record was so clean some people even said it squeaked.

"Emma, what do you need now?"

"Just your autograph. These are the papers we talked about. Read 'em over. If you have questions, call me. If not, sign at the X's and mail them back to me. I was coming out to see Mom, and just thought I'd bring these by to save you messenger fees."

"How considerate," he said with ear-to-ear grin. "Tell your Mom 'Hello' for me."

"Will do. By the way do you remember anything about Zunker Chemical?"

"A little bit. They had a plant down near Thompsons. Never did know what they made. All hush-hush and top secret. They had some sort of a spill, and the EPA tried to shut 'em down, but Hays Chemical bought 'em out. They had some sort of chemical process that Hays wanted. Never did re-open the plant. Just another example of too much damn government. Why do you ask?"

"Just heard that Hays may be having some EPA trouble of their own."

"Haven't heard about that. How's Bill doing? Don't see him much."

"He's fine. I'll tell him you asked. I better get over to Mother's. See you next quarter."

"Bye now."

As she left Emma said to herself, "The last time I talked to Mother, she thought she was fourteen and in high school, but we'll see."

In response to Emma's knock on the back door as she entered the house, Angela, the long-time maid and Emma's nanny said, "Emma, come in. It is very good to see you."

"How's Mom doing?"

"*Lo mismo.* Some days worse than others."

"So what's today like? Good, bad, or twenty years ago?" Angela made a non-committal face.

"Come on back with me to see her."

"O.K., but if she doesn't know who I am, I'm outta here pretty quick."

Emma's mom sat upright in the bed, covers pulled to her waist. "How are you?" questioned Emma.

"Fine. Just sitting here waiting for my date. We're going to the Prom. I'm the only freshman girl invited. I'm so excited."

Emma turned around and headed back to the kitchen.

"Angela, you take such good care of her. She's so clean, and her hair looks lovely." Emma was sincere. Angela did take very good care of her mother. It wasn't Angela's fault that her mother had destroyed herself with booze. *No, only one person was responsible for that*, Emma thought bitterly.

"Thank you, Miss Emma. You remind me so much of your mother when she was young. You are both so beautiful and so trusting. You both believe that everything good will come to you if you follow the rules. That is why it is so sad. She had not been drinking the day she was driving and your brother was killed . . .

but everyone assumed she was drunk at the time. The rumors, they killed her soul. The drinking got worse . . . if everyone believed she was a drunk, why not be one? It killed your father's love for your mother. He poured out all his love on you. I hope that if you ever face disappointment, you will not drink like your mother. I'm sorry. I should not have said anything, but you look so like her, and I worry. You are doing very well. You are strong." The older woman patted Emma's shoulder.

"It's all O.K. I hope you are right, about my being strong," whispered Emma as she touched her lower abdomen. *I hope I am strong enough to make someone pay.*

Hays Chemical was one of the largest chemical companies in the world. Home-based in Delaware, its Texas operations had been set up during the Second World War. Proximity to the Texas oil fields and a year round deep-water port on the Texas coast had worked well for the firm. After what Samuel Cox had told her and seeing the plant the day of little David Jess's funeral, Emma was growing more certain that some chemical leak had caused the mutation that all these people from Richmond had. And even though it wasn't affecting the parents, the carriers, it meant that when they had a baby . . . O.K., she wouldn't dwell on that. It damn sure *was* affecting the carriers.

Emma called the number listed on the sign that she had jotted down. Within minutes Emma was speaking to the human resources person at the plant. "My uncle William worked at a plant near Richmond, Texas, one that Hays bought a number of years ago. The plant's closed now, and Uncle William is in a nursing home. Anyway, he wanted to get in touch with some of the people he used to work with for old time's sake. Do you happen to have a list of the employees who used to work there?"

"No, ma'am. That used to be Zunker Chemicals. We just bought them for the rights to a chemical process they had developed."

"Why did they close the plant?"

"I don't exactly know ma'am. I heard that they had had some sort of a 'spill' and killed some cattle on neighboring farms. Zunker was really eager to sell."

"Were any of the employees hurt in the 'spill?'"

"No, ma'am. Everybody checked out O.K. The community was kinda concerned. We bought all the dead cattle and much of the land surrounding the plant. That's pretty standard procedure, without admitting any guilt, of course. We had the animals tested at A&M. We brought in all the proper state and federal agencies and made sure our clean-up was done properly. We have a clean bill of health from the EPA for that land.

"Like I said, all the employees were checked out by a doctor in Richmond. Zunker was in way over their heads. That's probably why they were eager to sell. Even before the 'incident.' I don't think they were that well managed—brilliant scientists, but not good managers. It takes a lot more than good science to create a successful chemical company. Zunker had actually closed the plant before Hays bought it. All the employees were retired or laid off. Hays didn't pick any of them up. They were never Hays employees. It took us a while to turn the public sentiment around, but we did," he concluded confidently. "I know this story pretty well. I was handling PR in those days, and this represented my first negative impact situation. The first one where I was on the inside looking out so to speak."

When he paused, Emma realized why he didn't need time to look up the plant before he took her call. She hadn't given the receptionist anything except her 'uncle's' name. No, he must have been trained about how to respond to any inquiries on the Zunker plant when he worked PR. They must have had lots of inquiries, or they were very afraid of any that they might have. A company as big as Hays must have frivolous lawsuits all the time.

His responses cheered Emma. She was on the right track.

"So how would Uncle William talk to someone who would know where some of these people are? Was there a union or something? Who has the records?" Emma tried to sound like a compassionate niece trying to help ease the last days of a beloved relative and not like someone pushing for information.

"All the records on the plant were kept by a local lawyer in Richmond . . . name of Smithers, Jason Smithers. Anyway he might be able to help you. I hadn't thought about that place in fifteen or twenty years."

"Do you know what was made at that plant?"

"No, ma'am. And even if I did, I couldn't tell you. It was top secret then, and it's still classified today." He was even smoother back on the more common questions. Emma spared a passing moment of sympathy for the Hays corporate attorneys. They were besieged on every side, it was about to get worse, and they had to depend on people like this Jason Smithers as their first line of defense.

"You wouldn't happen to remember the name of the doctor in Richmond, would you?" Emma asked.

"Funny, but I do remember. Seems like it was Coleman, yeah, Jess Coleman, M.D. Really nice guy. Had a rich wife that drank like a fish. I think he died. Well, if I can do anything else for you, let me know. But do it quick. I retire in two weeks . . . been with the company forty-three years. And the last thing I'm gonna want is to keep in touch with the people I've worked with," he laughed

"Thank you for your help." Emma got off the phone without even having to give a fake name, and since she was calling from the Kinko's near her house, even caller ID wouldn't have helped, but it didn't seem like the personnel professional was concerned about her. She hadn't enjoyed the characterization of her parents, but she couldn't refute it.

So Jason Smithers was the attorney that Hays kept on retainer to handle these Zunker Chemical inquires, Emma thought as she drove back to her home office. *And he was in Richmond. I've never heard of him, which was all the better,* she thought. She would get online and find out more about Mr. Smithers, what he owned, any news stories about him, lots and lots of information. When she met him tomorrow, even if he happened to recognize her, she would still know more about him. It always paid to be more knowledgeable than your opponent.

Emma and Daphne drove to Richmond the following day. Richmond started out as a small town about thirty miles south of Houston, even before there was a Houston or even Allen's Landing. Even as Houston grew rapidly, a small gap still remained between the two city limits. A norther' had blown in and cleared the skies. The temperature had dropped at least twenty degrees from the day before making it a gorgeous spring day.

Daphne said, "Tell me about Richmond. I'm a big city girl so this small town stuff is really foreign." Always good to distract Emma from thinking that now would be a good time to dictate a brief or filing or merely work on their to-do list.

Emma answered, "Here's the history lesson on Fort Bend County and Richmond. It was founded in the 1820s by some of my ancestors. Momma can trace her family back to the Old Three Hundred, the original settlers. Richmond was really named for Richmond, Virginia, but now people play up the ties with Richmond, England—a smaller city on the River Thames. They talk about the parallels between Richmond, Texas, on the Brazos River and Richmond, England on the Thames. Just more putting on airs and trying to pretend that Richmond, Texas, is something.

"When I was growing up, I thought it was a small town full of hicks, and nothing has happened to change my opinion. That, and my father's insistence that I leave, is why I got the Hell out of Dodge.

"You haven't suffered the confines of being from a small town," she continued. "Everyone knows everyone else. No one buys a new car, paints their house, or goes on a cruise without everyone hearing about it. It's awful; everyone knows everyone else's business."

She thought about it for a minute, and then continued, "And you are trapped exactly where you started out. You can't go anywhere in anyone's mind."

"What do you mean? Where you started out?" Daphne asked, not understanding at all.

"I was always Jesse Coleman's daughter, the doctor's daughter. Everyone knew that my mother had a drinking problem. Only Daddy showed up at anything requiring parents. I always felt ostracized or weird because almost everyone else had two parents, but even the ones with a single parent had a mother. I had Angela at home to help me with my clothes and things, but that didn't make up for school functions and things. And the thing that pissed me off the most was that my mother was in the same place she is today, in bed, drunk. I think the fact that everybody in town knew the situation contributed to Dad's encouraging me to leave Richmond. I guess Richmond could have been O.K. for someone else, but the part I didn't like was that everyone knew everybody else's business. I always felt like I was always on display, wherever I went in town that they were just waiting to see if I was more like my dad or more like my mother."

With surprising insight Emma said, "I started out in college as a pre-med major. I think that was mostly to please my dad, but also to show everyone that I was more like him, and almost nothing like my mother. After he died, I got to thinking about what I really wanted. I wanted to be recognized for what I did. And, I wanted to make a lot of money. So, I checked into law school. I still got a Biochem degree, so that no one could say that I changed because I couldn't cut it, but I added some other courses, and here I am.

"I think it really bothers me that something from here can still reach out and fuck up my life, like this has."

"What's the deal with this chemical plant?" Daphne asked, glad to move away from the very personal topic that she had stumbled onto. "Do you think that spill had anything to do with this problem? What did that plant make anyway?"

"One at a time. In reverse order, the plant was always real hush-hush. Nobody would ever say what was made at the plant. Rumors were that some sort of toxic nerve gas was produced there. Toxic nerve gases can produce mutational changes in chromosomes.

We know that everyone involved with the defective births has chromosomal abnormalities. So it's possible that the 'little spill' did more than kill cattle. We'll see if the company's lawyer can give us any information. I couldn't find the name of Jason Smithers in the phone book. But I did find where he was on the tax rolls and that he went to South Texas to law school. Graduated a while ago, so he will be in his sixties. We'll check at the county clerk's office in Richmond; they'll know where his office is."

As Fort Bend County had gotten the overflow of people from Houston, so it had obtained a growing number of Houston's legal problems. The legal complex in Richmond, the county seat, consisted of a lovely three-storied courthouse built in the early twentieth century. It had been well restored twice and looked so good that it had been used in numerous movies and T.V. shows. Two county office buildings had been built much later. They were built for room with little if any thought given to style or appearance. A large multi-storied jail housed those waiting for or who had received justice. The county clerk's office had been converted from a combination filling station and hardware store. Surprisingly it looked good and was very functional.

Emma and Daphne approached a cute, dark haired Hispanic woman behind the counter. "How may I help you?" she said.

"Can you tell me where I might find the law offices of Jason Smithers?"

"Oh, I don't know. I've only worked here six months. Ruth," she called to an older, heavy-set Anglo woman, "Do you know an attorney named Jason Smithers?"

Ruth walked over slowly. "Jason Smithers is dead. Right before he died he sold his practice to Jon Miller. His office is on Front Street."

The first woman grinned, "Oh, man. He's a hunk!"

Ruth grinned too, "Adelina, you know you're not supposed to talk that way about the attorneys. But," and she smiled sheepishly, "Adelina is right on."

Emma smiled back, buying time "Tell me more about this

Adonis." She was rethinking what she had learned about Mr. Smithers, scrambling to handle the change.

Ruth, once started, was eager to play historian, "Jon, or more correctly, Jonathon Miller moved here eight or ten years ago and bought Jason Smithers's practice at that time. Jason had just won the biggest case of his career and with all the money he made, decided to retire. Jon Miller was looking to relocate. His brother had just been elected judge for the District Court in Victoria, and Jon didn't feel like he could ethically practice before his brother . . . and he is a stickler for ethics. Anyway ol' Jason died about two weeks after he sold out.

"Mr. Miller does mainly civil law . . . estates, divorces, wills. Occasionally he'll do some minor criminal cases. Most of the big crime he refers out.

"He's in his thirties . . . never married but dates a lot. I once heard him call himself the 'County's Cheapest Rent-a-date.' He went to Tulane for undergraduate . . . degree in History, I think. I understand that some of the unmarried cuties from New Orleans come to Houston just to look him up. In fact there is one over there that always asks him to Mardi Gras every year, and he always goes. He did law school at Baylor. He always says he wasn't sure what he was doing in Waco with all those Christians."

Emma laughed, "Maybe he has political aspirations?"

Adelina said, "I first met him when he bought my champion rabbits at the county fair. He bought them at the auction and then gave them back to me. He even judges some of the Lamar Consolidated High School FFA projects." Clearly Jon Miller had won her over as he seemed to have the rest of the Fort Bend County Clerk's office.

Ruth winked, "He's a real cool dude just like Ferris Bueler. Anything else we can do for you?"

"How do we get to his office?"

"Down the street two blocks, hang a right, and it's the second house on the left. Big white wooden house converted into his law office. There's a sign in the front yard . . . you can't miss it."

"Thanks," Daphne added, as she turned to follow Emma out. *I'm gonna have to tell this girl about catching more flies with honey than vinegar,* she told herself.

"Daphne, I need to stop off at the library for a minute before we go meet this 'cheap date' guy. His name sounds familiar, but I can't place it yet. Let's go see what he owns and if he gets his name in the paper," she explained as she headed to the Albert public library for internet access.

If two women, one black one white, dressed in business attire drew looks or even comments, they didn't notice. "Being retired and dead explains why I couldn't find much about Smithers. Let's just see if I can't do better with Jon-boy." First she called up the Texas State Bar site. "There's so much information you can learn about who people are, but most people don't take the time. Aha, here he is—member in good standing of our prestigious association. He's a couple of years older than I am, and he went to Baylor law school, as advertised. And," she continued after a few more clicks and a little typing, "he owns the building his office is in on Front Street. Ha! He even owns a house here, as I can tell by his listing in the phone book. The county appraisal district values the house at $127 K and the office at $189 K. Not too shabby."

Daphne was looking over Emma's shoulder. "He's doing O.K. if these are both him. We'll have to wait to see what we think of the office. Now, let's see how he's doing in the community," Emma said as she went to do a search on the local newspaper, *The Richmond X-ray.*

Just as they had said in the county Clerk's office, there were several mentions of Jon Miller, local attorney, purchasing FFA prize winners. "It's not the Houston rodeo, but he's doing something. So far, he lives up to his advance billing. No pictures, but darn, his name still sounds familiar. Guess it wasn't work related or you'd have remembered him, Daphne. Let's go meet him and see if he's as attractive as they say, or if he's just benefiting by comparison with the usual county clerk's office traffic." Emma cleared the screen of her searches and ran a couple on the local football team for the next person to find.

Daphne nodded, not sure what she had agreed to, but it seemed to be what her boss expected.

"If you 'google' me, you get my listing on the law review and the articles I did for *The Houston Post* about tax law. No, Google doesn't show anything on Mr. Miller that we don't already know about him or his association with Hays. I'm ready; let's go meet this 'rent-a-date' gigolo."

Daphne was surprised at the casual sneakiness that seemed to be appearing more and more often with her boss. Oh well—nothing even close to illegal or unethical—nothing straightforward either. Guess she had always been this way, but usually the opponents were corporations, and Daphne couldn't help but worry that this was all very personal with Emma. And that might not be good.

CHAPTER 10

Back in Emma's car, they drove by a number of older houses that had been converted into offices and commercial use around the court house. The white clapboard house was easy to find on Front Street. Daphne read aloud the sign in front, "Law Offices of Jonathan Miller, Esq." and below that "Diego Villanueva, *Abogado*, Atty. at law."

They walked up a curving walk bordered by red and white cyclamen. A small sign above the door handle said, "Enter Without Knocking," which they did. A short, thin woman in her mid-forties sat behind the reception desk. Her ponytail looked as if it were pulled too tight causing her eyes to protrude.

"May I help you?" she said, looking as if each word required a monumental effort.

"We'd like to see Mr. Jon Miller if he is available. My name is Emma Anderson. I'm an attorney in Houston, and this is Daphne Armstrong, my legal secretary."

"Do you have an appointment?" Another monumental effort to get the words out.

"No. We were just hopeful he might work us in."

"I'm sorry, but he's not in right now. He's out running with Cato. That's his chocolate lab, named for the Green Hornet's faithful companion. They usually run in the morning, but he just got back in from a trip to New Orleans. Truthfully both he and Cato are pretty testy if they don't get their run in.

"You'll have to pardon me," the woman dragged out the words. "I have thyroid problems and have been off my thyroid medicine for a month prior to some tests. I feel like I died, and they haven't buried me yet. I'm Maureen, Mr. Miller's secretary."

"My mom has to take thyroid pills," Daphne said sympathetically. "When the dose is right, she feels fine—otherwise!"

At that moment the front door opened, and a "real hunk" in sweats entered. "Maureen, I just put Cato out back and noticed he's out of food. Could you remind me to get some when I leave this evening?"

"Mr. Miller, this is Emma Anderson, an attorney from Houston, and Daphne Armstrong, her legal secretary," Maureen told the man.

"Did I forget an appointment?" he asked, turning toward Emma.

"No. We were trying to see Mr. Jason Smithers. I understand he's dead, and you took over his practice. Say, haven't we met? Our firm's Christmas party at the River Oaks Country Club?" Emma extended her hand.

"Guilty as charged," he said with a smile that accentuated his deep dimple on the right. "How can I help?" he asked, shaking her hand. He had recognized her, too, but he wouldn't have placed her without her help. He remembered Grace's spiteful remarks and wondered what she would be like in a completely professional setting. She seemed more focused than he remembered.

"I'm looking for information about the old Zunker Chemical plant down at Thompsons. I understand Mr. Smithers handled their work before Hays Chemical bought them out. My Uncle William worked there. He's in a nursing home over here on Jackson Street. He wanted to contact some of his old co-workers for old time's sake before he died. The person I spoke to at Hays Chemical said you might have an old list of employees."

"All that shut down years before I came here. If you can give me a couple of days, I'll see if I can find anything. Mr. Smithers was none too good about records. Call me day-after-tomorrow, and I'll let you know what I've found." They exchanged cards.

Daphne smiled goodbye to Maureen as Jon and Emma finished up.

Later in the car, Daphne exclaimed, "That man is a 'hunk.' This case is looking good, girl."

"Yeah, and small time guy like that, he doesn't even realize there is a case. Let's see how much we can get before he figures it out."

Two days later Emma returned from a hair appointment to find her voice-mail light blinking. "Jon Miller here. I dug through the archives and found a list of people that Zunker sent in withholding for. I don't know any addresses. They probably wouldn't be any good anyway. Let me know if you want the list faxed, e-mailed, or sent in by messenger. You can pick it up any time if you're in the neighborhood. My number is 281-555-2334."

"Jon Miller, Attorney-at-Law. How may I help you?"

"Maureen, this is Emma Anderson. We met a couple of days ago. Mr. Miller left a message for me saying that he had found a list of names for me. If I came by this afternoon, could I pick it up and talk to him just a minute?"

"Sorry, but he's in court all day today. He says somebody's got to pay the rent. You can pick the list up from me, or you can come by tomorrow. The morning's totally free after his run with Cato," she explained.

"I'll see you in the morning," Emma said and hung up.

Going against traffic the trip to Richmond sped by. Emma circled the courthouse and then made her way to Front Street. At a little after ten, she was walking up to the door of Jon Miller's law office.

"Hello, Mrs. Anderson. Jon just called. He's on his way back and will be here in about five minutes. Come on into his office. Care for a Coke, water, coffee?" Maureen asked politely.

"Nothing for me," Emma answered, looking around the office.

The office was done in a rich wood paneling. The rug was a deep blue. Two leather chairs faced an impressive desk. Jon Miller had a tall, leather chair behind the desk. On the other side of the room a set of four chairs was placed around a dark wood coffee table. One wall was filled with the usual law office books and journals. The wall behind the desk was covered with diplomas and plaques, including his diploma from Baylor Law School. There was a large color picture of two young children, a boy about seven and a girl about three. One wall contained the largest collection of mystery novels Emma had ever seen. She took one or two of the older volumes down and found that they were signed by the author.

"Hello! Sorry if I've kept you waiting. I'll get the list." Jon Miller said as he bounded into the room.

"No problem. Good to see you again."

"Here's the list. I looked it over and didn't see anyone with the name 'William' so I don't know if it's a complete list."

By then Emma had the list in her hands. To cover her fake "Uncle William," Emma quickly looked down the list and found the name "Henderson W. Williams." "I think he used his full name 'Henderson W. Williams' for legal purposes."

"Anything else I can do for you?" Jon asked. Jon's radar was picking up on more than the usual big firm arrogance and disdain for small town attorneys.

"Do you know what they made out at the plant?"

Jon replied, "Not really. I know the product was covered by national security laws. So even if I did know, I'd have to kill you if I told you," he said with a big smile. "Anything else?" *As a fishing expedition, she wasn't doing much good. Surely if a firm like hers had an interest in Hays Chemical, they were on a first name basis with the in-house attorneys. Why would she bother with me?* he wondered. *This was getting interesting. I love the unusual and it's been slow since Mardi Gras. I'll have to check with Grace to find out what was going on with Mrs. Anderson.*

"I heard you weren't married . . . who are the lovely children in the picture?" With that comment, Jon's senses went on full alert. And he remembered what Grace had said at the Christmas party when he first met Emma—Barbie and Ken Anderson, that's what Grace had called them. Fake, arrogant, and, as he was seeing first hand, condescending. Well, he could play the good ole boy with the best of them.

"Those two are my favorites . . . they're my brother's kids, and I love 'em to death. I get to spoil 'em rotten and then leave. Living here I don't get to see 'em like I did when I lived in Victoria . . . but with my brother being a district judge there, I thought it might get sticky. You see, I'm a very ethical bastard . . . laid-back, yes, but always ethical. Anyway they're less than two hours away, and they visit me during the summer." He poured on his drawl and even managed to use his body language to appear slightly mentally slow. He had picked the photo up and was gazing at it to keep from letting Emma get too good a view of his face during his performance.

"What's with all the murder mysteries . . . I've never seen so many." Emma asked, glancing around the office.

"That's my only vice. I like to read an author enough 'til I see how he or she thinks. Then I play a game with myself to see how many pages before the end I can figure it out. Most authors don't put in irrelevant facts . . . so when you see something that seems irrelevant, bam! It's probably the case breaker. What do you read?" Jon asked, hoping to learn more about this woman he was beginning to suspect would be confronting him in the near future.

"Oh, I don't have time for fiction. My job is really demanding, and, of course, I read quite a bit during the day. I haven't read any fiction since I left Rice."

Jon smiled to himself at how easily she worked the name of her alma mater in. This lady was a piece of work.

"I left Richmond before you arrived. If I'd have known you were coming, I might have stayed." Emma smiled at him with a subtle invitation. "Thank you so much for the list. I may have more questions later." She had turned and headed for the reception area before Jon could reply. She took the list and her Mercedes and returned to Houston.

"Feel free," he said to the empty office. *Wonder what that was all about*, he thought, as he dropped down in his desk chair. And he looked up Grace's phone number in his rolodex.

"Cato, come on in here, boy, and leave Maureen alone." The dog loved to sit with his head in the secretary's lap and have her pat him. This arrangement didn't allow her to get much done, and Jon suspected that she was just the slightest bit afraid of Cato. He picked up the phone to call Grace as Cato arranged himself noisily at Jon's feet.

Jon was glad that Maureen had the dosage worked out for her thyroid medication and that she was back to being herself. He didn't particularly like that she said he and Cato got testy, but still, it was good to have her back.

CHAPTER 11

The next morning as her secretary settled in to work in the temporary office Emma said, "I've got your first task directly related to the chemical spill. Here's the list from the plant, and here's a Rosenberg-Richmond telephone directory. See if you can find anyone. Look under the names. Check all the nursing homes in the area. If you find anybody, see if we can set up interviews."

"I'll let you know what I find," Daphne replied and began thumbing through the phone book.

"In the mean time, I'm going to do some leg work in Richmond. Everybody has water bills . . . don't know if city hall will be helpful, but we'll see. And, I'll check with cleaners . . . everybody has to get their clothes cleaned. I'm going check some of the coffee shops and restaurants, too. Everybody has to get a cup of coffee now and then. If the waitresses have been around a long time, they may know somebody. They'll be much more likely to answer."

"I'll call the local undertakers . . . they may have planted some of these already," said Daphne.

"Good plan," called Emma as she shut the door behind her.

Emma wheeled into the driveway of her West University Place home about five o'clock. She and Daphne had set up an office in the smallest of the four bedrooms of the house. They each had a phone and a desk. They shared a computer-fax-copy machine. Emma bounded up the stairs. "What have you found out?" she queried.

"They've planted most of these people. The funeral home people are very nice and informative, and the phone company sucks. I've got appointments set up tomorrow with two . . . one lives with his son and the other lives in a nursing home in Richmond. Five I can't find doodlie on," Daphne summarized.

"The water department sucks, too . . . 'we can't give out the names or addresses of our customers because of privacy rights.' The guy at the cleaners knew all but about three of the people. You're right, most of them are dead. Five have moved to heaven knows where. Let's compare lists." said Emma.

Cross checking the lists left only two names unaccounted for. One of them was Henderson W. Williams, interestingly enough.

"What time are the appointments?"

"Mrs. Emerson at the nursing home at ten and Mr. Jenkins at his son's house on Long Drive at two."

The next morning Emma and Daphne pulled up behind the Richmond Golden Years Nursing Home. "How do they have the gall to come up with these names? I mean The Golden Years?" laughed Daphne. The building was about thirty years old, made of brick painted yellow, which they probably thought was gold. Green fungus had a good foothold although some attempts at removing it were evident. The gagging fragrance of urine with its ammonia residue and body odor greeted them at the door.

"We'd like to see Mrs. Emerson, please. I'm Emma Anderson, and this is my secretary, Daphne Armstrong. We called yesterday."

The lady at the reception desk was wearing a blue, all-purpose seersucker coat about three sizes too large for her. The word "Volunteer" was written in dark blue thread above her pocket. She looked old enough to be a permanent resident.

"Mrs. Emerson," she said spinning a rolodex on the desk in front of her. "Ah, yes. She's in twenty-three A, the bed nearest the door. Down that hall, third room on the right." She stared at the two as they headed off.

They found Mrs. Emerson, a pleasant-looking seventy-plus matron, sitting in her bed, looking at a small T.V. set on top of the dresser across the room. In the other bed lay an old, black woman on her side, facing the wall and snoring loudly. "Mrs. Emerson, I'm Emma Anderson. This is Daphne Armstrong, my secretary. We'd like to talk to you about the plant where you used to work. Would that be all right?" Emma unconsciously spoke louder when her first words got no response.

Even in her loudest tone, there was utterly no response; no change of expression. Even the roommate snored on. Mrs. Emerson didn't even blink. Emma repeated her introduction several decibels louder. Still no response. They returned to the reception desk and told the volunteer. "She hasn't spoken a word since she came in here two years ago. She had a bad stroke, but she doesn't look like she's hurting." Emma and Daphne beat a hasty retreat.

"Why the Hell didn't she tell me about Mrs. Emerson yesterday?" Daphne asked as they got back in Emma's car. "Did she *want* to waste our time?"

"Who knows what goes on in the minds of the good citizens of Richmond, but you may have spoken to another volunteer—one who has never seen Mrs. Emerson before."

"Are you gonna try to contact some of Mrs. Emerson's kids or relatives?"

"Don't know. I only need one witness to point us in the right direction. Let's see how the next interview goes. I know it's kinda early, but my stomach says it's lunch time. What say we grab a bite to eat before we go see Mr. Jenkins?"

"Sure."

There were two small restaurants in downtown Richmond. One had been a bank and the other a feed store when Emma was growing up. They chose the old bank that now sported an Italian motif and menu. Over shrimp and fettuccine Alfredo, they discussed their wasted morning. "It would be much easier if we had more to go on, some plant records, but I think we're making progress," Emma said, more in a pep talk to herself than to Daphne. "If we don't get more from Mr. Jenkins, we'll have to take a different approach."

"Let's hope he's still all here," Daphne said.

"What's Mr. Jenkin's address?" asked Emma.

"Eleven hundred Long Drive."

"O.K., time for another Richmond history lesson. Do you know anything about Jane Long?"

Shaking her head, Daphne said, "You've got to be kidding. Never heard of her. Who was she?"

"Jane Long is called the 'Mother of Texas.' She's buried in Morton Cemetery here in Richmond. In 1820, she joined her husband, Dr. James Long, at an outpost on Point Bolivar, across from Galveston. Her husband left her, a twelve-year-old servant, and their six-year-old daughter, to go to Mexico."

"Sounds a lot like my husband. Except I don't think he went to Mexico," quipped Daphne.

"Jane Long vowed to remain at the fort until he returned. Unfortunately he got killed in Mexico City. On December 21, 1821, during a record ice storm, she gave birth to the first white child born in Texas.

"Later on, she ran boarding houses in Brazoria and here in Richmond. Pictures suggest she looked ugly as sin, but she must have had something 'cause some accounts say she knew Sam Houston, Ben Milam, William Travis, Stephen F. Austin, and Mirabeau B. Lamar, all heroes of the Texas war of Independence. Many historians say that 'knew' was in the Biblical sense of the word."

Daphne nodded with understanding, "Single moms had it really rough back then."

"After she died the town named lots of things after her, this street, an elementary school, and a couple of subdivisions. She was a strong willed ol' gal who certainly didn't have an easy life, but who didn't give up either at the first sign of trouble."

Emma thought silently for a moment. "Seems like Jane Long lost one of her babies, too," she said quietly under her breath. *There'd been a lot of strong, determined women during the establishment of Fort Bend County,* she thought. *Dammit, they didn't give up, and neither will I.*

Promptly at two, they pulled up in front of James Jenkins' home on Long Drive. The house was a 1970's style ranch surrounded by numerous live oak trees. Petunias and hibiscus filled the flowerbeds in front. Mr. Jenkins answered the door himself. A sprightly man in his mid-eighties, he invited them to take seats in a conversation area in front of a large fireplace. The fireplace was not lit; in fact the air conditioner was on. "What can I do for you two ladies?" he said after they had introduced themselves.

"Did you work at Zunker's Chemical Plant down at Thompsons?" Emma asked going directly to the topic, very relieved at his obvious mental competence.

"I did indeed. Best job I ever had. I made a good wage and had health insurance on top of it. I was really sorry when Hays closed it. Went to work for the county in the water sanitation plant. Stayed there 'til I retired. Get a good pension from Hays. And get one from the county, too." He chuckled at his financial success.

"What did you make at the Zunker plant?" Emma asked, hoping that she didn't have to explain her interest. She didn't; Jenkins seemed pleased to have someone interested and willing to listen.

"We weren't ever told exactly what we were making. Just that it was very toxic. We had very strict safety rules that were tightly enforced. Break a rule and you were out of there. We had to wear masks, rubber gloves, and rubber aprons. Most of the people had to wear goggles. They used crude oil directly out of the Thompsons fields. They actually had a little pipeline to carry the oil from the well to the plant. They stored the product in large steel oil drums, and they shipped the barrels out to the military once a week. They had some trouble with the stuff eating through the steel drums, so they shifted to plastic. One time a couple of barrels sat out over the weekend and leaked out all their contents. That's when a bunch of cows grazing nearby died. Zunker owned right up to the problem. Got all the governmental pollution people in and did a massive cleanup. Sent us all to see Dr. Jess Coleman to get checked out. Say aren't you Dr. Coleman's daughter? He had a daughter Emma who would be about your age. Real pretty gal . . . little wild though. She always drove a Corvette. She sure was her daddy's favorite."

"Yes, I'm that Emma." Don't volunteer anything, Emma

reminded herself. It's the first rule of courtroom questioning. Only answer the specific question asked.

"Thought you were. Anyhow Hays bought them out shortly afterwards and closed the plant."

"Was anything wrong with any of the employees?"

"Nope. Your dad said everything checked out fine."

"Any problems show up in later years? Any more cattle die?"

"Nope. Hays had all the cows tested at A&M. Said they all died of poisoning. They incinerated all the cattle. Hays bought up a lot of the surrounding land at a good price. Nobody complained about nothing. The old plant's still there, but nobody's been in it for years."

"Do you know the whereabouts of any other former employees?"

"I think old Ms. Emerson is still alive over at the nursing home, but she had a bad stroke and doesn't talk any more. Most everybody else is dead or moved away. Anything else? I'm supposed to go play golf this afternoon with Widow Ellison. She's not much at golf, but she does a mean pot roast, and if I'm good, sometimes I get to stay the night."

Daphne had to look away to keep from laughing at this elderly playboy.

"Thank you for your time, Mr. Jenkins." Emma stood and carefully didn't make eye contact with her secretary. It really wouldn't do for both of them to break out laughing in his face.

Back in the car, Daphne rolled her eyes, "Man, I'd hate to be a shareholder in Hays Chemicals after the court awards you total ownership."

"Oh, yeah." Emma felt more optimistic than she had since she first went to Dr. Wornat.

Daphne boarded her bus and headed home when they got back to West U.

The flashing light on the answering machine caught Emma's attention as soon as she walked into the room. She picked up the phone and entered the code. "Jon Miller here. I need some information from you. What's really going on? I found some more paper work on the plant including pictures of the employees. Henderson W. Williams was black. What's your game? I don't like being jacked around. Call me. You have the number."

By the time Emma heard Bill come in the back door, she had had plenty of time to run lots of scenarios about how to respond to the phone call from Jon. Things had been getting increasingly tense between the Andersons. Bill wanted to try again to have a child. "Look," he said, "the chances are one in four that we have a bad outcome, and we had it. We ought to get a free ride on the next one."

Emma explained to him, "It doesn't work that way. Each pregnancy was a one in four chance regardless of the previous pregnancies." Emma still had not gotten over the discomfort of the last pregnancy and the mental anguish of the birth or termination as Dr. Wornat called it.

Emma continued with, "I want to sell this house. It's got too many bad memories." He chalked up the talk about selling the house to hormones, and now he tried to focus again on their original plan. It had actually been Emma's plan, so he knew she would come back to it.

Emma told him, "I want to tell you what I've found out. I listen to your shit . . . your cases, your sports stories, and tales about the dumb asses you work with. Now listen to me! I want the bastards who caused our problem to pay. I want to file suit. Tell me if you think I've got enough information." Emma was so enthusiastic about what she had learned from Jenkins that she ignored Bill's comments on having another baby. She still hadn't called the realtor, but as she grew more confident about the case, she moved filing for divorce higher on her list. The financial award, especially for pain and suffering was going to be hers. Bill obviously hadn't suffered like she had, so he shouldn't get any of the money.

After hearing what she had discovered about the plant, the toxic materials, and the dead cattle, Bill said, "I don't think you've got a case, unless you can find out what they made at the plant and whether or not it causes mutations. Also you'd have to show how we got exposed. Too much of your case is your supposition of what happened."

"I've asked the attorney who bought the practice of the actual attorney for Zunker Chemical what was made at the plant, and he blew me off. Hays Chemical won't tell me. They keep hiding behind National Security."

"I think without that information you'd be hard pressed . . . unless in discovery you could force their hand or make them slip up and admit something. How bright is this guy in Richmond who has all the records? You think he might spill something inadvertently?"

"You've met him. Remember Grace's 'rent-a-date' at the firm Christmas party?"

"Not really."

"Well, it's the same guy. Right now I think he's pretty bright. I thought he was pretty laid back, but he's already caught me in a lie." Then she told him about her "Uncle William."

"Oh, shit. Sounds like you royally fucked this up. Does the firm know you are doing this?"

With Bill's words echoing in her ears, Emma slammed out the back door and drove off. "I don't need to be told I fucked up by a junior associate lawyer from a second-rate law firm," she muttered.

A couple of days later, Emma agreed to meet Bill for dinner. They arrived separately at a Thai restaurant in the shopping area called the Village.

"Babe," said Bill stirring his after-dinner cup of coffee, "I don't know why you can't put all this behind you. Why can't we try again? The doctor said there's only a one-in-four chance that this will occur. We've had our one. Look at that couple out in Leakey you told me about . . . they had two normal kids.

"Also, it's awful expensive paying on our house and everything with only one salary. Why can't you just get over this, go back to work, and get back to our normal life?" Bill had thought that a two-pronged attack based on Emma's past motivators was the way to go. He had planned the dinner to be the first step back to normalcy.

"You bastard. You don't understand what I've been through... you don't know what it's like to give birth to a deformed baby boy that dies! How can we lead a normal life? We're not normal, and we don't know what caused the problem or who is to blame."

Bill paled at the mention of the baby boy. He was too shocked to say anything.

"And if our house is too damn expensive for you, let's sell the fucking thing . . . in fact, why don't we quit this whole fucking marriage?"

Emma couldn't mean that, Bill thought, still speechless.

"I'll file for divorce tomorrow and call a realtor in the morning. I'll tell you when you need to sign the papers. Now you better stay the Hell away from me!" Emma ran sobbing from the restaurant.

She didn't wait for morning to call the realtor. Silvia Earl, the wife of one of the partners that Emma really liked, ran a very successful real estate company. Emma called her from her cell phone. "Silvia, this is Emma Anderson. How are things going? Listen, I'd like to list our home in West U. with you. Bill and I are probably splitting up . . . anyway that place has bad memories. I'll fax you the information about the house along with a floor plan first thing tomorrow."

"Sorry to hear about you and Bill. I always thought you were too smart for him." Silvia didn't get to consistently be the top realtor in her office without being able to read people. She could tell from the tone of her voice that Emma had already ended the marriage in her mind. It seemed pointless to discuss an already finished deal. "I'll take a look at the stuff you fax me . . . my fax number is 713-555-1776. Then I'll call you about price, showings, etc.

"You certainly have a classic West U. home. Nothing to turn anyone off. How are the interior colors?"

"I went with wheat grass throughout. The dining room is

a dark clover green, very classic. But it is almost the only room like that. There aren't any special wall treatments or anything like that."

"Great. I'll run some comps, and we'll talk about the strategy for asking price tomorrow."

"O.K."

"Does Bill know? Who can I tell?" Silvia was eager to share her gossip, but not at the expense of ticking off her client.

"Yes, Bill knows," or *he does if he was listening* Emma thought. "You can tell anyone who asks, but don't offer information. And thanks." She closed her cell phone. One detail down; nine hundred and ninety-nine to go. She'd get Daphne started on some more of the details tomorrow. She paid the firm for Daphne's time; they didn't care how she used it.

"Hey Grace! What's up?" Jon asked. He hoped that she was another woman, like Maureen, his secretary, who knew copious amounts of information about people even when she claimed she didn't know much. He had debated making this call, concerned that Grace would interpret it as a more personal interest than anything else, but he needed to get a handle on his opponent.

"Jon! I haven't heard from you in a while. Not much is going on . . . just the same old same old. What can I do for you?" She was pleased to hear from him, but aware that he had called for a specific purpose, not just to chat. He would return a call, but he didn't initiate a conversation without a purpose. She might work it into something, like dinner or a date, but first things first. *What did he want?*

"You remember 'Plastic Bill and Emma' you introduced me to at the River Oaks Country Club? Is she still working for your firm? I ran into her out here at my office in Richmond the other day. She said her uncle worked for a firm that my predecessor represented before he died. So I kinda inherited the files. Anyway she was nosing around for information . . . and it seemed strange. I can't believe that your firm would be interested in a defunct chemical plant." He hoped that praise of the firm and Grace's dislike of her colleague would be enough to get some information.

"Emma has gone on a modified FMLA plan, but she has kept a few clients," Grace replied. "I think that foundation down there is about the only client she kept. I don't know anything about an uncle. I'm sure we represent some individuals, but . . ." The implication was that any individuals important enough to be represented by the firm wouldn't be Emma's personal clients.

"What do you mean by a modified FMLA plan?" This was going O.K. Grace certainly kept up with the other members of the firm.

"The Family and Medical Leave Act of 1993 allows you up to twelve weeks of leave for a pregnancy, etc. Well, 'Plastic Emma' negotiated a nine month leave with no salary. She kept a few clients active, and she is paying Daphne's salary and benefits to the firm. Daphne is assigned to Emma for the duration. Oh, yeah, Daphne is the super black lady who has been Emma's legal secretary since she started at the firm.

"Listen, give me a couple of days and I'll see what I can root up," Grace said. This way she had an excuse to call him back.

"Talk to you then. And, Grace, thanks," Jon was continually amazed by people who knew many details of other's lives, and were open to learning more. *I must be reading too many mysteries and not paying enough attention to the world around me,* he thought.

A couple of days later, when Maureen was out, he got the call. "Jon, this is Grace, calling back with my spy report," she laughed.

"Hey, thanks for calling back. I really appreciate your help. I don't like not knowing what's going on with the opposing counsel, if that's what she is. You know what I mean?"

"Yeah, I don't like being in the dark either. What we've got here is a classic 'I'm smarter than you and the rules only apply to you and not to important people like me' Emma. Emma is still on leave.

DEE WILBUR

Daphne is working for her full time, and Emma is reimbursing the firm for her salary. The Albert Foundation is the only client for sure that she's kept active, and nobody knows for sure what else's going on," Grace summarized her information concisely.

"Is Daphne a nice looking black woman in her early thirties?" he asked, making sure that there were no mistaken identities. The stranger this got, the more careful he would be.

"That's Daphne. She's really smart with a good sense of humor," Grace added. "Wish she were my secretary. She can really get things done."

Grace continued with her report. "There is one rumor floating around the firm. I can't confirm it, but the wife of one of the partners sells real estate, and we've heard that the 'plastic Anderson's' house is on the market. I don't know if a divorce is in the works, but I wouldn't doubt it. If they do go splitsville, Emma will be the one to file." She seemed smug about the news.

"Wow!" exclaimed Jon more in appreciation of Grace's investigative skills than at the mention of a divorce. "You are truly amazing, like my secretary Maureen. You guys know more 'stuff' about people than I know people. I'm sorry the Andersons are having problems, but I don't see how it could have anything to do with Zunker Chemical, Hays predecessor.

"Me either. Who knows what goes on in that woman's mind. Hey, my literary club is having a dinner-dance on St. Patrick's Day. Any chance your Rent-a-date service has an opening for you on that date? I'd love to have you go with me. I promise not to make a fool of myself like I did at Christmas," Grace added.

Here comes the tricky part, thought Jon, *putting her down firmly but gently.* "I'd really like to go with you. I still remember your talented tongue even if you don't. But I'm kinda committed. Shit, I'm totally infatuated. The engagement isn't official yet, but I'm hoping. She's a wonderful lady from New Orleans . . . and I guess you could say she's closed my rent-a-date service. But thanks anyway." He hoped she would accept his refusal, uh, gracefully.

"If she's in New Orleans and you're here, she'd never know." So much for gentle acceptance.

"But I'd know . . . and you know I really am an ethical bastard. Truly, thanks for the offer. You're a very attractive lady, and you shouldn't be wasting your time on a rental service anyway," Jon said. *But you're not Sandy. I want Sandy and I want the world to know that Sandy is mine.*

Jon and Cato had just returned from an evening run when the phone rang. "Hey, Shyster. I just needed to talk to somebody. Dad's in the hospital with pneumonia. He started running fever and coughing two days ago. I couldn't get him to see anybody until this afternoon." Jon could hear exhaustion in her voice, and it worried him.

"Do I need to come over? I can be there in about four hours, especially at this time of the evening."

"No, the doctor said that he'll be fine. He'll probably only be in for a day or two, and then I'll take him back to his apartment. They have twenty-four-hour-a-day nurse coverage there so somebody will be able to look in on him around the clock. I just wanted to talk to you," she said, settling in to do just that.

"O.K., I can talk. I can do whatever you need me to do. I've got this weird thing going on over here. I told you about the lady lawyer I met at the big Houston law firm's Christmas party? Well, she's checking out the defunct chemical firm that used to be south of here. The one Hays Chemical bought out. I got the inquiry because the guy I bought the practice from used to represent the defunct chemical company." He really could tell a good story when he put his mind to it. And now he set out to distract her from all thoughts of doctors and hospitals.

"Anyhow, she's asking about the plant and what it made. I don't know what's going on. I talked to another lady lawyer at that same firm and found out she's on some type of modified family leave. I truly don't know what's going on." Jon knew that distraction was one thing, but mentioning his opponent's divorce would be something else all together—it would be stupid.

"That second lady lawyer wouldn't be the one you had a date with for the Christmas party, now, would she?" Sandy asked, confirming his suspicions that she was extremely aware of all the other women in his life, no matter what their role. And he couldn't think of a single downside to that. He simply needed to turn her awareness into a willingness to wear his engagement ring.

"Yes, it was, oh green-eyed one," he answered with a chuckle.

"I am not jealous, only curious," she protested.

"Well, actually she invited me to a St. Patrick's Day dance..." It was probably cruel and possibly self-destructive, but he couldn't resist teasing her a bit.

"And what did you say, counselor? Be careful how you answer."

"I told her that I appreciated her invitation but that I was involved with someone very special, and though the engagement wasn't official, I was hopeful that it soon would be. And I am right to be hopeful, aren't I?"

"All in due time, my dear."

"Then, just when I thought I had handled it beautifully, she said that if you were in New Orleans that you'd never know." Jon finished in a rush. *Definitely self-destructive.*

"And what did you say? Be careful, you're doing well so far." Sandy was smiling now that she had turned the tables on him, or that he had turned them on himself.

"I told her that I would know, and that I was a moral and ethical bastard, so thanks but no thanks. How was that, my lady love?" he asked.

"A good answer, sir Jon, I love you more that you will ever know . . . but right now I have all I can say grace over with Dad. I can't think about anything else right now, but you do have right of first refusal," Sandy explained.

"I know. You hang in there. I'll be here if and when you need me. Now, get some sleep. Sandy, I love you. Call me tomorrow and let me know how your dad is doing. Good night." He realized that Sandy loved her dad and that she truly was overwhelmed. Jon reasoned that a little patience now would gain him points in the long run. And he wanted Sandy for the long run.

Jon wondered how he could help her. You didn't send flowers to a man in the hospital with respiratory problems, and who knew when she would be at her apartment to get a delivery. Flowers were out. Pizza, he could send her pizza at school for lunch tomorrow. Of course, in New Orleans, he would probably end up with crawfish po'boys, but food was it. Now, what was the name of that little hole-in-the-wall restaurant right on the corner across from the school? Jon fell asleep thinking of po'boys and Sandy.

CHAPTER 12

After the blow up with Bill and the call to the realtor, Emma had gone to a motel that night and turned off her cell phone. The next morning she called Daphne and asked her to watch her house and to call after Bill had left for work.

"As the weather man said, 'The coast is clear,'" chuckled Daphne as she saw Bill drive off. Emma arrived home about twenty minutes after Daphne's call.

"We've done everything I can think of short of filing a federal request under the Freedom of Information Act to get something from Zunker. Looks like I'm gonna have to get Mr. Rent-a-date to tell me something."

With a quizzical look, Daphne asked, "And exactly how are you going to do that?"

"I don't know, I just don't know, but I'll think of something. Call him and set up an appointment, today if possible."

"Couldn't hurt to try."

Daphne called and made the appointment. Emma wasn't sure what to say, but she believed when all else failed, mount a full frontal attack. As Daphne headed down to the firm's offices to file some Albert Foundation papers, Emma headed to Richmond. On the drive to his office, she went over her approach. She had to give him the outline of the facts, but she didn't need to admit to any wrongdoing that he didn't already know about. He could probably save Hays a lot of money and be a hero by negotiating a settlement without letting it go to trial where they would bring in someone else to litigate it and have him just sitting there. *Yes,* she thought, *that would be the key to Jon—money for handling the case; praise for the quick, quiet resolution.* She had chosen a business suit, but one in a deep rose to keep it feminine. The blouse was light but not sheer. Not her most conservative suit, but one that was definitely feminine.

Emma entered the front door of Jon's office. Maureen looked up at the sound of the door, "He's here; head on back. He's expecting you. Need something to drink?"

"No thanks, I'm fine."

Jon motioned her to a chair. "To what do I owe this visit, Mrs. Anderson?"

"I have been less than candid with you. For two months now, I've been trying to find out what killed my baby and several others."

Holy shit, Jon thought, but he didn't say anything.

She continued, "I gave birth to a baby boy who died immediately after birth. He lived only a few moments. He was born with a condition called rachischisis, which means the spine and brain fail to fuse. It occurs when both parents have a certain mutation on their thirteenth chromosome. Statistically one out of four of their children will be affected."

Feeling that he had to say something, Jon said, "I'm very sorry for your loss, but how does this affect Hays?"

"This genetic mutation," she continued, interrupting him, "can be caused by several things. I have researched the incidence of this and found an unusually high occurrance center in Richmond and around the old Zunker Chemical plant, where they made a highly toxic and mutagenic product."

"Your research includes exactly what?"

"It includes the recognition that the parents were all exposed to the agent during the leak of material that killed the cattle, shortly before Hays bought Zunker. And you know how this liability works, just like the environmental cleanup. You go back to the original cause and follow it to the current owners and assigns.

"Enough of us were exposed and have suffered the lethal and tragic effects for the declaration of a class-action suit."

"And how many people would that be, Mrs. Anderson?"

"At this point, I can offer a dozen, but if it goes to trial, I expect that number to grow. I mean look what happened with Vioxx. The flood gates may open."

Jon listened quietly, saying nothing. When Emma stopped, Jon spoke very quietly, almost in a whisper, "I believe in justice, and I'll fight for the underdog . . . but I expect not to be lied to. I'm very sorry for what has happened to you, but I don't see how you can say Hays or Zunker is at fault. You don't know what the material was that plant produced or what it did or can do. Just for the sake of argument, how do you think you were exposed to this material?" Emma was surprised that he had focused so quickly on the one weak spot of her case.

"I don't know all the details. I suspect that it happened during the leak that killed the cows. Maybe I went to a picnic out there. The men were probably exposed during baseball games or practice. Bill's dad coached, and Bill and one of the other men played ball. The fact remains that Zunker and Hays *de facto* admitted to poisoning the cattle. I'm sure Hays doesn't want all the properties of this killing agent to become public knowledge—like how long does this stay active in the soil it spilled on? They want to quietly test the soil at intervals and avoid any mention of a possible Love Canal.

"Jon, Zunker killed my baby and those of other Richmond area parents. I spent months waiting for my baby to be born, only to have him die. He's buried here, near the thing that killed him. My husband and I cannot have another child—what kind of fool would risk another child dying? The other couples have children that are carriers of this lethal mutation. Someone has to own up to this destruction, all these lives destroyed. Hays destroyed my son and my marriage, and they are going to damn well pay."

Taking a deep breath and hoping for calm, Jon focused on the one ray of hope in what she had said, "If it goes to trial, I thought this might be the courtesy visit to tell me that you had filed on my client."

"No, I wouldn't file without talking to you. And I apologize to you for lying about my uncle, Henderson Williams, but I thought it was the only way to find out about the toxic, mutagenic crap," she pleaded with tears in her eyes.

"When that didn't work, which I assume it didn't because you haven't filed, what did you decide to do? Decide to proceed without any facts?" His patience was gone and his temper might not be far behind it. *How dumb does she think I am?*

"I approached the problem with the foremost expert in this area, a doctor in Houston. I am well connected here in Richmond and did the necessary leg work, that any good attorney would do. You would have done the same thing, Jon, if your baby had been murdered and your marriage destroyed."

"Umm," came the non-committal response.

"That's how I know you'll appreciate as an attorney and as a member of this community, why I came to you. This will be very, very ugly . . . inflammatory. No corporation needs that, especially not Hays."

He wondered briefly about her comment about "especially not Hays," but quickly returned his full attention to her. This was the climax of her discussion. She was finally going to get to the point.

"That's why an out-of-court settlement works so well for everyone." She stopped and waited for his response. His poker face masked any reaction.

"I want to see all the information you've got in your files on the product, Zunker Chemical, and Hays Chemical. You know I'm right. Let's work together on this, and Hays will be very appreciative that you made this go away with no publicity and for a lot less than a trial would have cost them," Emma concluded dangling her bait.

"You know I can't show you that. First of all, I'm still retained by Hays to handle anything having to do with Zunker. Secondly, the nature of the product is still classified. I checked yesterday. No information can be given out concerning that product without governmental approval." Jon felt some relief to know finally what Emma was after. *And,* he added to himself, *if you think that Hays would be happy with any kind of settlement, no matter how sealed, you have another think coming.*

"I really can't help you, even if I wanted to."

At this, Emma's patience snapped. "Oh, you could, if you really understood how things are. But I'll convince you, Hays, and a judge if you force me to." Emma turned to leave. "Someone is going to pay, and it's going to be a lot more if you won't work with me." she said. "Don't get in my way. I only know that I've been wronged. I've had to carry this deformed baby that's died, and it's killing me. My marriage has broken up, and I can't concentrate on my job. Dammit, somebody's gotta pay for this." Jon followed her into the outer office.

After Emma had slammed out without saying anymore to anyone, Jon said, "Maureen, you've lived here a long time. What do you know about Emma Anderson and her family?"

"Not much. You sure seem to tick her off. That's not the best you can do for professional courtesy, is it?" she asked. He shook his head, sadly.

"Point taken, now what do you know? You always know everything about everybody."

"Oh, I know her maiden name was Coleman, and her father used to be a G.P. here. I know her mother is a drunk. And I know that they are very wealthy. If you want to know more than that, you need to talk to Shannon Barton." Jon wondered briefly how much Maureen could tell him about someone she did know, if this was 'not much.'

"How do you know so much about so many people? And when will I know even a tenth about some of them?" he asked.

"Remember when you first bought the practice how I would sometimes suggest that you personally take some of the papers to the district clerk's office or the county clerk's office? It wasn't because I minded running the papers over there. They needed to get to know you, and you needed to get to know them. Then, pretty soon you'll know as much as I do," she explained, not that it was any clearer to Jon how she remembered all the facts or even ever heard them.

"That's why you sent me out to that first FFA auction, wasn't it? Maureen, I think that the most valuable asset I got when I bought the practice was you."

"Thank you," Maureen preened slightly. She thought so, too.

"Now, to demonstrate why I need you so much, who is Shannon Barton and why do I want to talk to her?"

"*He's* the editor of the paper," she emphasized the pronoun. "He's been here forever and used to be real chummy with the doctor. Wasn't he one of the guys you went duck hunting with last year? You know the one that almost blew your head off? He owes you one."

"Oh, yeah. I soiled my britches on that one. O.K., I'm off to buy a paper. Cato, you stay here." The lab made his disappointment clear with a loud sigh as he lay down.

"Shannon Barton, remember me? I'm Jon Miller," he said as he entered the small cluttered room in the back of the paper's offices a few minutes later.

"Sure I remember you. First time I was ever glad that I missed. What can I do for you?" The man behind the desk stood to shake Jon's hand. The editor was a medium man—medium height, middle aged, and a medium-sized middle section spread. He motioned Jon to a chair and sat back down.

"I need to know about the Coleman family . . . not the unabridged version, *The Reader's Digest* version will do nicely. I've encountered Mrs. Emma Anderson, formerly Emma Coleman, and I need background as to how seriously to take her in a professional capacity."

"Take her seriously. She always gets what she wants," the editor said without any hesitation.

"As for the family, the mother was descended from the Old Three Hundred, lotsa land, lotsa oil, lotsa money, and an unquenchable thirst. Some say she's the town drunk, but I don't think so. I think she is probably the most enabled drunk in town. Her first child was killed in an auto accident; mama was probably DWI. Emma came along a coupla years after the boy was killed. Kinda surprised people that they'd have another baby, that they'd put another baby at risk. Word was that Doc slept down in his library after Emma was born. Mrs. Coleman hasn't ventured from the house much after the boy's death. There's someone who lives in and takes care of Mrs. Coleman," he continued.

"Doctor Jess Coleman was the salt of the earth. Good doctor with a huge practice. Women loved him . . . said he was the most gentle doctor in the world. He was active in all the local civic groups. He gave the city the land for the big park down by the river. He paid for the lights for the little league park. He totally spoiled Emma . . . gave her a Corvette when she was in high school and a new one when she went to college. Paid for Emma to get a 'boob job' when she graduated from high school." Jon wondered if anyone didn't know Emma had had 'them done.'

"Oh, yeah, he was a big stamp collector . . . first day covers. He did this back before they had the services to do this for you. He'd get a list of where the first day covers were being sold. Then he'd make up an envelope addressed to himself, always with a letter inside the envelope . . . so he could say it was really used for postage. Then he'd seal the envelope and put it inside another envelope addressed to the postmaster where the first day cover was issued. He'd enclose enough money for the stamp, and the postmaster would affix the stamp and mail it back to him. They gave his collection to the Albert Library here in Richmond when he died of a massive heart attack.

"Emma was a gorgeous girl . . . kinda wild. She went to Rice, got herself a baseball jock for a husband. He went there too. I think they both went to U.T. Law School. I think they live in Houston.

"That'll be fifty cents please. The unabridged version costs two dollars," he said with a chuckle.

"Thanks for the info, and more importantly, thanks for missing.

Guess I got my fifty cents' worth," Jon said. He had plenty to think about and some work to do.

Emma and Daphne were working in the second bedroom of the apartment Emma had rented after moving out of the house with Bill. "Explain to me again why we made this move? I mean hauling all this office crap from your house to this apartment and setting up a new office. The view from the fourteenth floor is great, I love not having to change buses, and I could certainly get used to the 'luxurious apartment lifestyle,' but why are we here?"

"Look, the real estate agent said that emptying a third of the furniture out, but leaving the personal mementos, was the best way to move the house. You know the agent's husband is a partner in the firm with me. I think she is pleased to have the listing commission but even more pleased to be on the inside of the juicy gossip of the breakup of our marriage. I wonder how many people the bitch has told. But, she's the best at selling so I'm gonna do it her way. If it doesn't sell, it'll be her fault."

Bill was still in the extended stay hotel, trying to convince himself and Emma that this was just temporary and that things were O.K.

Emma spoke to Daphne and to herself, "Let's review our status. We've filed suit against Hays in District Court and are waiting for a trial date. We've written Hays asking for information about the Zunker Chemical plant and the products made there. We've written Jon Miller asking for access to the records of Zunker Chemical. We've written to the Secretary of Defense, the Secretary of Homeland Security, and the Secretary of Health and Human Services, OSHA, and the EPA. We've gotten several polite letters back saying that this information is classified and cannot be released and a couple that said, 'It's none of your fucking business.' You have any ideas, Daphne?"

"I wish you hadn't pissed off Jon Miller. He seems like a nice guy that might have let something out . . . besides that, he's a hunk."

Daphne got a glazed look in her eyes. "We could do some 'late-night discovery' at Miller's office, if that's where he keeps the records."

"Only Perry Mason can do that and keep his license to practice law."

"Even he uses Paul Drake," Daphne said, somewhat disappointed. Working with Emma, Daphne had really bought into the righteousness of their case.

"But your 'late night discovery' has given me an idea of something to do before I petition the court to force them to disclose."

"Jon Miller here."

"Jon, this is Emma Anderson. I'd like to discuss the possible release of any information about Zunker Chemical. There may be something that isn't subject to national security. I'm coming out to Richmond to see my mother Thursday evening. I wonder if you could come by and chat for a few minutes? I'd even buy you a drink."

"I've got choir practice that night from seven until nine. Would nine be too late?" Jon carefully kept his voice very even. He didn't trust Mrs. Anderson, but now that her inquiries were official, he wanted to follow all the rules in any dealings with her.

"Great. Mother lives on Hillcrest, number seven-seven-seven. It's the two-story red brick house with the large oak trees in front. See you after nine, Thursday." Jon finished the call and headed to his court date.

A couple of hours later, the door flew open with a crash, and Jon bounded into the office. "Maureen, Maureen, justice has triumphed once again! You will get paid this month. I will get paid. Life is good."

"What happened? Why aren't you in court?" asked Maureen.

"The Crawford Insurance Company settled. Mrs. Gutierrez got seventy thousand, and we got thirty. We were eyeball to eyeball out in the hall waiting to go into the court-room, and they blinked. Please deposit this check," Jon chortled, waving the check around, finally presenting it to her.

"Listen, Maureen. Since I don't have court this afternoon, I'm going to Thompsons and see the site of the alleged exposure. I found the keys to the place in one of Smithers's boxes. I'll be back by four or four-thirty. You can get me on the cell if you need me." He left with the same speed and energy level that he had arrived with.

"Drive safely, Jon," she called after him.

The road to Thompsons, a two-lane asphalt strip, ran through the Brazos River bottoms. The rich, black soil kept the foliage a deep green even in winter. Traffic was light, and Jon stepped up his pace. He checked his watch and saw that it was too early to call Sandy. She was still in school. Jon loved the T-bird on the freeway, but out here, with the whole road to herself she could really show off. But he wanted to share his fun with Sandy. With the temperature in the mid-seventies and with nary a cloud in sight to mar the beautiful blue sky, Jon pulled over onto the shoulder and stopped the car. Following the instructions exactly, he shifted into neutral and pushed the buttons on the dash. With the top down, he decided he needed his shades. *You know,* he thought, *a hat with a colorful band and a small feather might look good,* as he got back up to speed.

Several small towns dotted the highway: Crabb, that once elected a twelve year-old boy mayor, and Booth, named for one of the Old Three Hundred families, were two of the larger. Neither one had a population of more than one hundred. Thompsons had been an oil camp for Gulf Oil. At one time it had several hundred residents. It even had its own elementary school. Now all but two of the houses had been moved away. The streets, street lights, and stop signs were still all in place. It was like a scene from *The Twilight Zone.*

Jon crossed the railroad tracks paralleling the road into Thompsons very slowly to avoid any damage to the 'Bird. He drove the short distance to the gate blocking the road. The key fit and he opened the gate. The road deteriorated past the gate, so he continued on foot. The plant was a metallic building about sixty by forty feet. There were windows on three sides of the building. A lot of pipes still ran from the building, but they were all truncated and sealed about three feet from the building. A loading dock extended into the crumbling asphalt parking lot in the rear. Over the front door, the name Zunker Chemical could faintly be discerned. Sun and weather had almost eliminated the name.

Four plastic barrels sat on the loading dock, each properly labeled with a hazardous waste sign. A form on top of each barrel in a transparent sleeve listed the contents. This was the refuse from the locomotive service in East Texas waiting to be taken to the Hays plant on the coast for disposal.

The second key worked on the front door. To the right stood two small offices, vacant of any furniture. Two restrooms sat on the left, separated by a water cooler, now filled with dust and dead bugs. The hall opened up into one large room in the back. Four long tables, the kind in high school chemistry lab, filled the near end of the room. Sinks ran the length of the table with reagent shelves above the sinks. Each table had separate gas jets.

Overhead banks of fluorescent lights hung from the ceiling. Along one wall were numerous hooks, presumably where the employees hung their aprons. Lockers lined the immediately adjacent wall with an emergency shower at each end. At the far end of the room sat a very large stainless steel structure which looked as if it had a capacity of several thousand gallons. Various pipes entered and left this large tank, some disappearing through exterior walls. At the back of the building, there were two doors, one on either side of the room, separated by what looked like a conveyor belt. This was wide enough to carry large barrels. The largest pipe from the tank stopped above the conveyor belt, capped by a large metal disk. Jon looked around approvingly. Simple but workable. Whatever the product consisted of was mixed in the large tank and piped into barrels that moved along the conveyor. Barrels came in one door off

DEE WILBUR

the loading dock, were filled, and exited to the loading dock by the other door.

The building was still in good shape. The floor had been recently swept. All the windows were intact. Hays ran a tight ship. *No peeling paint or oozing noxious green goo—why was it always antifreeze green,* he wondered?

Jon mused, *Could this innocent looking place be the site of disaster? Am I putting any kids Sandy and I might have in danger? Naw,* he reassured himself, *Hays wouldn't expose an attorney, that's too much risk even for them.*

As he locked the front door, he noted something moving on the parking lot. He walked over and bent down to look . . . There was a small frog moving forward in a very ineffective way. The frog had three back legs. *Well, damn,* he thought. You didn't have to be a Ph.D. geneticist to know that the frog had problems—big problems.

After locking the gate behind him, Jon drove back to Richmond. The sky was still free of clouds, but a few clouds of doubt were gathering in his mind. *O.K., Watson,* he thought in his best Sherlock Holmes voice, *what do you make of the plant? That frog—a coincidence or one more clue of genetic abnormalities?*

Watson, never of much help to Holmes, was of no help to Jon. *Guess we better find out more about these frogs, Watson. We'll start with Bob Clark at choir practice.*

Jon thought back over his day as he sailed down the two-lane road. *A big settlement in one case and some more avenues to pursue in another. Not a bad day at all. And, a really great ride in the country—really a pretty good day.* All he lacked was his lady love to share it with.

Thursday evening after the rehearsal ended, Jon caught Bob Clark, a Ph.D. biologist who worked for Houston Power and Light. "Bob," said Jon, "I was down in the Brazos River bottoms the other day, and I saw a frog with three hind legs. Weirdest thing I ever saw. Have you ever seen anything like that?"

"Yeah. They're showing up throughout the country. Nobody knows why. Most people blame pollution. Some say it's due to parasites. Since my job with the light company is making sure we don't pollute Smithers Lake, the source for our cooling water for the plant south of town, I've read quite a bit about the 'frog scare.' I don't know what to make of it. It's only the little ones, *Rana pipiens*. If it were the big bull frogs, it might be a boon for those fancy French restaurants that serve frog legs. Listen, gotta run. See you Sunday."

He pulled into the circular drive in front of the Coleman house. *Man, there must have been lotsa oil*, he mused. Even though Jon drove a new, retro Thunderbird, purchased after getting his fee from a really big settlement, he felt like someone hired to mow the lawn, not an invited guest.

Emma answered the door herself, "Mother has drunk herself to sleep, and Angela has gone to bed so you can speak freely without fear of being overheard." She motioned him toward a couch flanked by end tables with Tiffany lamps on them. *The entire room had been stolen from the set of The Cosby Show*, Jon thought.

"Name your poison," Emma called out from behind a wet-bar. *Well maybe not everything came from the Cosby set*, he amended.

Jon said, "I'll have a beer . . . any brand as long as it's cold."

Emma brought the drinks, and they sat at each end of the couch. "Jon, you have a reputation of having a strong sense of justice and of fighting for the underdog. Isn't there anything you can tell me about Zunker Chemical and its product? You've read what happened to at least three couples in the papers I filed for the lawsuit. I'm certain the toxic materials from the plant are to blame. I need help." *And these people need to pay*, Emma added to herself. She had realized that Jon's knowledge might be enough. Maybe she didn't need to see actual papers before going to court. Daphne was partially right, they needed to get hold of what Jon had, but there were several ways to do that. She had reworked her strategy since storming out of his office a couple of weeks ago.

"Emma, I'd like to help, but my hands are tied." He pushed the image of the deformed frog out of his mind. *Parasites,* he thought, *gotta be parasites.*

"Excuse me a minute, I need to freshen up," said Emma as she walked to the powder room door into the next phase of her plan.

After a few minutes, Emma re-entered the room. She was wearing a blue negligee of the thinnest silk Jon had ever seen. Jon looked at her perfectly formed breasts through the silk. All Jon could think was *Ol' Doc Coleman certainly got his money's worth.* The negligee stopped short, leaving her long graceful legs uncovered. It was all that Jon could manage to set his beer down without dropping the bottle. He hoped that he wasn't actually drooling. He stared and tried to remember that she was a woman with a mission, not a table dancer.

Emma whispered softly as she sat next to him on the couch, "I'll do anything to get that information, anything! You don't have to show me the files, just tell me. Talk to me, Jon." She ran a beautifully manicured finger up and down his thigh. Jon's pulse doubled, then kicked up again. He closed his eyes briefly and then turned to face her, putting his hand over hers to still it.

"Emma, you are extremely beautiful." He paused to remind himself of Sandy and all his plans for them. "And in that outfit you are as sexy as anybody I've ever seen. But," he continued after removing her hand from his thigh, "I told you I was a moral and ethical bastard. You're still married so it wouldn't be moral. You're the opposing counsel so it wouldn't be ethical. Thanks for the offer but . . . no thanks."

Emma missed him with the Tiffany lamp as he escaped through the front door.

He heard the crash as he climbed into the T-bird. O.K., now he knew how far she would go for this case. It was clearly very personal for her. Jon was pretty sure he had stopped her for tonight, but what would she do next? How badly did she want the Zunker records that were sitting in his office right now? Badly enough to try her hand at breaking and entering? He hoped that she hadn't staged the 'event' as a distraction while someone else was breaking into his office. He checked his cell phone—no missed calls, so unless they were able to bypass the alarm system, his office remained safe.

He headed straight to a wine storage facility in the Sugar Land part of Houston. He had seen their advertising from the freeway— "Keep your wine here, we're open seven A.M. until midnight." Well, he would see about that. The night manager had been very helpful when he heard of Jon's plight—his uncle, Uncle Hays Zunker, had died and left an extensive wine cellar. Jon, the executor, was looking for a place to store the bottles until they could work out the estate. Jon even bought six boxes to pack the wine in.

After renting the storage, finally fitting the boxes in the T-bird (even flattened they barely fit), Jon headed straight for his office. The cheerfully blinking alarm light and the undisturbed boxes on the floor relieved him greatly. *I'm probably overreacting* he told himself *but Good God, I never, ever expected the lap dance presentation I got. Who knows what that woman will try?*

In about three hours he had transferred the papers to the wine boxes, and left only a single sheet of paper in the original bankers' boxes that were labeled Zunker Chemicals.

He had told the night manager that his uncle had mostly reds. A good choice since reds had a longer life, and he might need to store the 'bottles' for a while if the case dragged on. And, the reds wouldn't be kept as cold, so the papers wouldn't be that awkward if he had to get them out to refer to. Maureen wouldn't get suspicious.

He really didn't want to explain to Maureen what prompted him to take such radical measures. *Not that I am likely to forget the sight of opposing counsel in her teddy any time soon. Aw, damn. I still would have to see her in court. Talk about an awkward morning after! I'll just keep my eyes on the judge and never look at opposing counsel.* He thought he was fairly clever with his uncle's name; now when they were labeled no one at the storage facility would question it. And, Hays wouldn't bat an eye at the charges for "off site storage."

Now, sweating in his office, having transferred all the papers to new boxes, Jon felt like he might be ahead of Emma on this case for the first time. It took him two trips from the office to his house to get all the full wine cartons moved. He would feel even better tomorrow morning at eight when he got the boxes safely nestled away at the wine storage.

It was one thirty when Jon dialed Sandy's number and heard a groggy, "Hello?"

"Sandy, it's me, Jon. Everything's O.K., I just needed to hear your voice, pretty lady. Can I talk to you for a couple of minutes?"

"Sure, hon, what's going on?" She sounded more awake already.

"You know I love you. I'm not great at this relationship stuff yet, but I'm practicing. Tonight I went over to confer with the other counsel, the crazy female attorney that I told you about on this Hays case. She had set it all up. Her mother lives here in town and that's where we met, at her mother's house. Hell, I guess I thought she had seen that she had no case without some information on the chemical product. But she can't get standing to get the information— it's a 'Catch-22.' Guess she figured that out. She probably doesn't have a case, even if she could see everything on the product, but she wouldn't believe that."

"Jon, what are you talking about? Did you meet with the attorney from Houston? Did she drop the suit?" Sandy sounded a bit anxious.

"No, darling, that's what I'm trying to tell you. First let me say that I did nothing wrong—nothing happened between us. And I called you right away. She didn't want to drop the case; she wanted me to drop my pants. Sandy, after I got there and sat down, she changed into a Rick's Cabaret outfit and came onto me like a table dancer." Jon took a breath, now that he had finally gotten the worst of the tale out.

"What? What is going on? Do I need to come over there?" Sandy was completely awake now.

"No, I explained that I was having none of it or her, for several reasons: you as the number one reason, my understanding of ethical conduct as the second." Jon wasn't sure that these were in priority order, but he knew they were in the right order for Sandy to hear them. "Add to those, she's married, divorcing but married. Then I got the Hell out of there. When I closed the door, she threw something glass at it. I hope it was my beer bottle, but I bet it was one of her mother's Tiffany lamps," Jon finished.

"Oh, Jon, how awful." Yes, this is what he needed to hear. It had been awful.

"Awful for you and for her," Sandy continued. "She must be very desperate." Sandy knew how much his ethics meant to him.

"Yeah, she must be. That's why I'm so late calling. I went to my office and repacked the records she wants so badly into wine boxes. I rented a wine storage unit, and first thing tomorrow they go into climate controlled storage. No one would think of looking for my Uncle Zunker's reds. I don't think Mrs. Anderson would have someone break into my office, but after tonight I'm not taking any chances."

"I should hope not. And don't get caught alone with her either," Sandy agreed. "I'm sorry this happened. Jon, I trust you, but I'm glad you told me."

"Funny, it was one of her shenanigans that gave me the idea of the name. She said that she was trying to help her uncle, a Mister Henderson, find some of his co-workers. He's an old black man that no one can find, and he is not her uncle."

"That's great, Jon."

"I love you, pretty lady. We can get married anytime you are ready, remember? O.K., go back to sleep. I know tomorrow is a school day. But the semester is over half way done. Soon, you can come see me!" This had worked out really well. Jon was almost starting to trust his instincts with Sandy.

"Love you too. And I can't wait until June. Bye."

They both hung up. Jon glanced around his bedroom and the shelves lined with even more mystery novels. Being here with Sandy was worth ten couch dances with Mrs. Anderson. *What was she, crazy? Was her mother crazy, too?* Jon hadn't smelled anything on her breath, but she certainly wasn't behaving rationally. *What would Sherlock Holmes ask Watson?* Jon wondered.

The next morning about nine, Jon sat in front of his office in the T-bird.

Gus, Maureen's husband, pulled his nine year old, dark green Ford F-150 pickup to the curb to let Maureen out. Jon jumped from his car and walked over "Gus, have I got a deal for you? I need to borrow a pickup this morning to run some stuff over to Sugar Land. Would you swap vehicles with me until noon? You take the T-bird, and I'll drive the truck."

"Have I died and gone to Heaven? Where do I sign up?" smiled Gus from ear to ear.

"I'll meet you back here at noon," said Jon, as he flipped Gus the keys to the T-bird and helped him from the truck.

Gus smiled, "Drive carefully with the truck . . . don't want no scratches on my baby. I got a real good deal on her. Green colored trucks don't sell too well around here."

It only took Jon about an hour to place the "reds" of Uncle Hays Zunker safely in storage. He didn't scratch the truck.

CHAPTER 13

Jon sat on the tall stool at the counter in the breakfast nook-kitchen. He was finishing his first cup of coffee for the day. After the rough couple of days he had had, he was getting a somewhat slow start. Cato lay on the braided rug just inside the living room. He was being patient this morning . . . since Jon had on his running shorts and jogging shoes, he knew that they were going for a run.

As he glanced around, Jon realized that he liked his house but that it would never do for a family or even a married man. It was too small. Sometimes even he and Cato were bumping into each other. And, no matter how much fun Sandy's little garage apartment was, small wasn't how he wanted to start out their life together. He had bought it mainly because it was in old, downtown Richmond and was over a hundred years old. It was too small, but it had plenty of history.

He had grown up in an old house in Victoria, Texas, when it was a small town like Richmond now. He liked the small town atmosphere. He even liked the fact that everybody knows everyone else's business. Many a time growing up, he had returned home after committing some small misdeed only to find out that when he got home, his mother already knew about it. Now he was trying to get more involved with the community; not because it would help his practice or because Maureen told him to, but because he liked being a part of things. Sandy would fit in nicely, and *soon,* he prayed *soon.*

The house was built before indoor plumbing; it had been built when kitchens were in a separate building because of the fire hazard and to keep additional heat out of the house during the hot months of the year. The house was two stories with dormer windows on the second floor looking out over beautiful old oak trees in the front lawn. The ground floor originally had a living room-parlor and a dining room. Originally there had been two bedrooms upstairs. A two-story addition had been cobbled onto the end of the house . . . this consisted of a full bath on the second floor and the small corridor-type kitchen, breakfast bar and a half-bath on the first floor with the kitchen replacing the formal dining room and extending into the new addition. With the shifting, gumbo soil in Richmond, he often worried about the two parts coming apart, especially when he heard late night creaking.

His bedroom was furnished in what might be called bachelor primitive. He did have a nice bed with a bookshelf headboard. For the first few months that he lived in the house, he had sheets for window coverings, but Maureen finally shamed him into buying some Wal-Mart curtains. He was still using college-law school sheets and towels. If he ever did win Sandy's hand, they would have to find something more suitable. Maybe he should make that clear to her.

"All right, Cato. Let's move it." Cato sprang to his feet with his tail wagging. Jon opened the door, and Cato waited at the curb to see which direction they would take this morning. It was just daylight and the commuter rush into Houston had not yet started so Jon elected to run around the YMCA ball fields, paralleling the Thompsons Highway. He and Cato then cut off onto Hillcrest, a street with very elegant homes. The lots were quite large, some being four acres in size. There was one older house that was built on the edge of a lot leaving about a two-acre plot vacant. Jon thought, *Wonder if a young, newly married attorney could convince the owner to split the lot? More significantly could a young attorney afford it?*

His reverie was broken by Cato's sharp barking. A squirrel had left the safety of its tree and was attempting to cross the road at ground level. Cato was in hot pursuit. Jon quickly dashed into the street to head off Cato. A pickup truck came to a screeching halt just inches from Jon. The driver, an older rice farmer that Jon recognized from church, ran down the window, "Jon, you better focus on what you're doing and not get tangled up in trying to figure out what the dog is up to. I realize when you're up to your ass in alligators, it's hard to remember that your job is to drain the swamp. But you could get yourself killed. Now be careful."

With that, he ran up the window and slowly drove off. The squirrel had made it to a large magnolia before Cato could catch it.

"This is Bob Duggan from Hays Chemical. May I speak to Jon Miller?"

"Just a moment, Mr. Duggan," Maureen said, before putting him on hold to tell her boss.

"Jon, it's Bob Duggan from Hays Chemical."

Great, Jon thought, *I wonder how Mrs. Anderson has tried to screw me over now. The attorney for the local region of Hays calling couldn't be good news. If they pull their account, I really will have to contact Purina.*

"Put him through."

"Bob, this is Jon. What's up?" He tried to sound optimistic, or at least calm. If he had gone through all the work to ensure that the papers were in safekeeping, and then they pulled the business- well, at least his last bill would have plenty of hours.

"We just got the papers on the suit filed by Emma Anderson. What is this shit?" Hays' counsel was not amused.

"A number of people from Richmond, including Mrs. Anderson, have had horribly deformed fetuses. The suit tries to lay blame on a leak at the old Zunker Chemical plant down near Thompsons. It was a long time ago, before I got to Richmond. You remember a bunch of cattle were killed. During the purchase of the process and the land, Hays acted very responsibly, calling in the EPA and all the other big boys. Nothing was ever found. That's well documented, and we're covered on that. I don't really know what they made down there, do you?" Jon was pleased with his review of the facts, and thought that if he could find out more than Mrs. Anderson knew, he might stay ahead. That is, if he was still on the case.

"No. I'm having some of the boys here look up details now.

I believe you have most of the paper work there. The attorney you bought out handled everything for Zunker. Anyway, can you handle this? All my troops are tied up. You know how we hate publicity. If you can keep it out of the courts, we'll give you a big bonus . . . otherwise two hundred an hour outside court; four hundred in court." Jon smiled. He liked the no-nonsense approach Hays took, and he liked what he knew of Bob.

"Yeah, I can handle it. We'll do what's seems fair. I'll let you approve any settlement if we have to go that way. I've had a couple of meetings with Mrs. Anderson where she has been doing anything she can to find out about the product. I don't think her case is very strong. Fax me what she filed and I'll start right now." Jon smiled again. This was working out O.K., maybe even fine. Now, if he could just win the case or convince the other side to drop the case, all without getting any adverse publicity, he would be fine.

"We also got an EPA inquiry about some barrels down at the old Zunker plant. Hays has a contract with East Texas Locomotive Refurbishing to get rid of some of their lead- containing paint. They put it in barrels and store it in the parking lot at the old plant. We truck it out on a quarterly basis," Bob continued.

"The EPA was satisfied with the contract. Apparently the guy who paints the trains is a real square-shooter. He hadn't had any fines from the EPA for three years prior to signing the contract. The conduct by Hays has also been excellent with no evidence of any danger to the environment, plants, or animals. Why we haven't even injured a human! Anyway EPA gave us a clean bill of health in writing. That's as good as it gets. Don't know who could have called the watchdog line."

"I wonder if dear Mrs. Anderson had anything to do with this? It sounds like something she might do," Jon commented.

"Listen, Jon, keep me informed."

"You got it, Bob." With that the line went dead.

Emma said. "I've filed a petition with the district court in Richmond asking it to force Hays Chemical and Jon Miller to turn over all their records to me. We've got to find the proof that the plant was making toxic chemicals or they get away with this."

Daphne looked up, "When will the judge hear your petition?"

"Next Thursday at two," Emma replied. "Just filing might shake something loose. Someone at Hays corporate may show better sense than Mr. Jon Miller," Emma said bitterly. "They won't want to go to court," she explained to Daphne. "Every news story, good or bad, drops their stock price. The last thing they want is more publicity, especially about babies. But," she paused her pacing mid way across the room, "we can't go to the press yet. I need a clear chain of events, probably the product name and some of its contents, like 'known cancer causing benzene' before I go to the press. I'm sure it was Zunker at the root of this, but I don't want any fancy footwork on Jon's part or on the part of their corporate counsel to give them grounds for a libel counter suit." Emma resumed pacing.

She turned toward Daphne, "Wonder when Jon will get the call that someone else is taking over? They won't let some small town lawyer handle something this big," she said.

"Bet he gets the call pretty soon," Daphne answered. She had seen the lawyers at the firm develop their trash talk strategies before, but she sensed a little something more in Emma's comments. Some spite? Sounds almost like Emma hadn't told her much about the meeting they had had. "He probably doesn't even know what they made at the plant—he's just holding the papers until Hays puts a corporate lawyer on it. He'll get dropped to second chair, if he even gets to stay around."

"We'll know on Thursday; they'll probably send both Jon and the new guy to see the judge. O.K., let's see what we need to do before Thursday."

The courtroom of Judge Thomas Carlson occupied a portion of the second floor of the courthouse in Richmond. The entire room was done in dark oak paneling. Six ceiling fans revolved slowly over head. A deep burgundy carpet covered the floor. Emma and Daphne sat at one table inside the railing separated from the visitors seats. Emma kept glancing over her should for late arrivals. Only Jon Miller and Maureen sat at the adjacent table. Judge Thomas Carlson was presiding. He was an older judge in his early sixties with long grey hair and bushy eyebrows. He was a no-nonsense type judge who did not like lady lawyers. Jon had been pleased about who was hearing the case.

Emma presented her case showing why she needed the information and why she felt entitled to it. Mostly a restatement of what the initial filing contained. "Your honor, with the records from the Zunker Chemical plant, I can have experts, medical experts, show how even very small amounts of the product could have caused this chromosomal damage . . ." She was interrupted.

"I object your honor," Jon stood slowly. "Mrs. Anderson doesn't even know what the product is, so unless she has a medical expert who will always say that trace amounts of anything can cause birth defects, she can't know this. She is calling on facts not in evidence. Ones that don't exist and will never be in evidence." Jon sat down slowly without looking at Emma.

"Objection sustained. I read the brief that you filed, Mrs. Anderson. I don't have any questions about the content. If you have anything new to add, please do so now," Judge Carlson instructed.

Emma was beginning to sense the Judge's animosity. "Thank you, your honor. The harm done by Hays is so great that it requires recompense to the victims, your honor. And the determination of how callous Zunker and its assigns Hays were in their disregard of the safety of unborn generations depends on the information in those records, your honor. Please grant the victims access. Thank you." With that, Emma sat down. She looked straight ahead at the judge, never glancing toward the other table. She couldn't believe that Hays had left Jon as the only attorney on the case.

Jon presented letters from the Defense Department and the Department of Homeland Security indicating that the information was still classified and could not be presented. He walked to the Judge's bench each time to hand him a copy of the letter. Jon indicated that he could get representatives from the two departments to come to Richmond if the judge wished. He stated that he was just trying to save money and time by having the letters instead of representatives. Emma objected strenuously, "I have a right to examine those people under oath."

"Ma'am, you're going to have to get your information some other way. I am not dragging two representatives from Washington into my court. It's the last thing that I want. I'm denying your petition. You may, of course, appeal. In the meantime, I suggest that both of you get on with discovery, and get your depositions done. This hearing is adjourned." With that pronouncement, Judge Carlson left.

Emma gathered her papers and walked out without waiting for Daphne or speaking to Jon or Maureen. She was so mad and, in an odd way, so hurt that she was about to cry. She went to the ladies room on the first floor to wash her face and pull herself together for the ride back to Houston. She wasn't accustomed to losing.

Daphne watched as Emma almost ran from the courtroom. She turned to Jon and his secretary. "This case means a lot to her. Usually she has a lot more support. I don't go to court with her. I'm probably not even supposed to speak to you, I don't know," she finished uncertainly.

"I know it means a lot to her," Jon replied. "I know it's personal, very personal, but I can't let her have the records. You heard the judge." He turned back to the table and helped Maureen gather up the remaining papers. "I suspect I'll be hearing from y'all," he said to Daphne as he left the courtroom with Maureen.

When they got back to the office, Jon went in to call and update Bob Duggan at Hays. His call was answered on the first ring, "Duggan here," Bob said briskly.

"Bob, this is Jon Miller in Richmond. I just got out of Judge

Carlson's court about the Anderson suit. It went well. He did not allow her to subpoena any Zunker records, which is good. She'll appeal, of course, but I don't think she'll get anywhere."

"Sounds like it's going just fine. What's your next step?"

"I was thinking that it would be good for me to have all of the information that we would want to provide ready. That way we are forthcoming with anything we can be, putting off any appearance of hiding something," Jon explained, getting ready to bring up the issue of the cows.

"O.K., but what in particular? There's really not much we can share, national security wise," Bob said.

"Where are the records on the cows that died and were tested? Couldn't we show that we are willing to give all the secondary information that we have?" Jon hoped that Hays could give him something to work with.

"I see what you mean, give them something. The testing was done at A&M, so I believe that you have all those records. Go ahead. See what they have. If they charge you something to go back through their files, fine. I don't think there's anything to worry about there, but if there is, we can deal with it when you find out. And that's better than having her force the issue."

"I'll check the records I have here. I'll let you know what I find," he said. "I'm mostly in wait mode, so I'll call you if I learn anything or if the other side makes any unexpected moves. Thanks." With that, Jon hung up.

Looked like he would be taking a trip to check on his uncle's wines before he went much farther. He headed out, telling Maureen he'd be back in a couple of hours.

Emma dutifully filed her appeals. They were promptly rejected. "Jon's probably a big contributor to the re-election campaign of the Appeals Court judges. It's a good ol' boy's club at its worst. Damn it."

Daphne wisely kept her mouth shut about the different political action committees that her boss supported at the insistence of the partners. She had heard Emma call it "the PAC tax," but that was clearly different.

Daphne had tried to distract her boss by offering to coordinate a lunch with Grace or any of her friends. Emma's response had always been the same, "Thanks, Daphne, but I don't have anything to talk to them about. And I can't believe that any one of them would have an inside track into getting information from Hays." Daphne had been floored. You didn't go to lunch with a friend to fulfill a specific task or topic. You went to keep in touch, to hear what was going on with her. Daphne had, with Emma's blessing, arranged to be in the downtown office on Wednesday mornings, to have lunch with a couple of her friends at the firm, then to come back to Emma's that afternoon. Emma's take had been that it allowed Daphne to keep up on all the news at the firm. She had completely missed the personal connection.

The morning after the last appeal was rejected, Daphne and Emma were in the office. "Daphne, I don't know what to do. The information exists. I know it does, but I don't know how to get to it. I'm almost ready to try a little breaking and entering." Emma was back to her pacing. "But you gave me an idea. Please find a list of Hays' outside counsel. Let's do some background on them, so when they switch attorneys, we'll be . . ."

Daphne interrupted, "I've been thinking. Didn't you say that your dad examined all the workers in the plant after the spill? Would he have put anything in the medical records? Where would his records be?" Daphne had been thinking about the case, mostly worrying about what her employer would do next if there wasn't some progress or at least some hope in the case.

"You're beautiful. Of course, Dad would have put something in the records. I'll be dipped in shit if I know where the records are. In Texas the medical records belong to the doctor although the patient is entitled to a copy. I'm sure Dad would have made some provision for taking care of his charts. Let's hope we can catch Mama sober enough to tell us. Maybe they're out in the garage or in the old store room behind the garage. I didn't pay much attention to them when I was handling the estate. Quick, let's run down to Richmond right now. I'd call ahead to see how far gone she is, but her condition can change by the time we get there." Emma was headed to her car before Daphne could turn off her computer and grab her purse.

CHAPTER 14

Emma pulled her Mercedes into the driveway of her mother's house. "We'll go in the back. Grab a Coke or anything you want. I'll be right back. Mother is iffy at best, but a stranger certainly won't help." Emma gave a shutter as she glanced in the living room on her way to her mother's bedroom and sitting room suite.

"Mama, it's Emma. How are you doing? Are you feeling any better?" she asked in her kindest voice. Her mother was always feeling bad, so it was a safe question to see how things stood.

"Who are you, and what do you want?" Her mother looked pale, but otherwise she looked wonderful. Her hair was clean and neatly combed. She wore a pink bed jacket over a very light blue granny gown. She was sitting up in bed with the comforter pulled to her waist. The T.V. played softly in the background. Emma could see that Angela was taking excellent care of her charge. Now, if she could just get her mother to answer one or two questions and answer them in the present, not fifty years ago.

"Mama, I'm Emma, your daughter. How have you been?"

"Who did you say you were?" the older woman looked at her questioningly. Today wasn't a good day.

"I'm Emma, your daughter. You remember me, don't you? You remember how we used to . . ." Her voice trailed off as she tried to think of a fun activity they had shared to jog her mother's memory.

Her mother interrupted, "Don't have time for much chit-chat. I'm waiting for my date. He's the quarterback of the football team. We're going to the prom. Going out to eat at Bill Williams restaurant before the dance."

Emma thought she would try to play along, "Who's your date?"

"Silas Snedecor. Nicest looking boy in school. Do you know him?"

"No, I don't know him. Momma you aren't in high school. You're a grown woman. I'm your daughter, and I'm a grown woman, too. Concentrate, dammit!

"Do you remember Daddy? He was a doctor."

"Of course, I remember Daddy. Why wouldn't I remember Daddy?"

"Do you know where Daddy's medical records were put? Do we still have them?" Emma asked.

"No, no, I'm going to the prom." The older woman became agitated, repeatedly checking her hair, fussing with her bed jacket, and looking around wildly.

"Miss Emma?" Angela had come into the room. She stepped over to the bed. She made a soft hushing sound as she handed her patient a magazine. Distracted by the bride fashion magazine, the older woman quieted.

Emma turned at the question. "Yes, Angela."

"Your daddy's records are all with Mrs. Matilda Jones. You know she was your daddy's nurse for at least twenty-five years. When he died, he had in his will to set up a fund to pay her for keeping his records. She was supposed to keep 'em for twenty years. She had to send copies of a lot of records right after he died. Bet she doesn't get too many calls for them now. She ought to still have 'em."

"Angela, I love you. I remember Matilda now that you mention her. Where does she live?" In her relief to have her questions answered, Emma ignored her mother.

"Her husband is a rice farmer, Mr. Ed Jones. They live out on Rice Field Road. They have been out there about forty years. They had three kids there. Now all of them are grown and left like you. I will draw you a map so you don't get lost and wander all around." Angela really did know everything, Emma thought, as she headed back to the kitchen to get Daphne.

Emma retrieved Daphne from the kitchen, and map in hand, they headed toward Rice Field Road, about seven miles south of Richmond. Emma was driving, which left Daphne to navigate. It wasn't hard to follow the map, so Daphne was taking in the scenery. The asphalt two-lane passed through flat farmland on both sides. "What's that big ditch we've been driving along for the last mile or so? Is it a bayou? Is it going to flood?" Daphne inquired.

"That, Daphne, is a rice canal. Rice fields have to be flooded with water to grow properly. They pump the water from the Brazos River into the canal. It then flows to the various rice farms. When you see those canals, you know you are in rice country. You really are a city girl, aren't you?"

They found the Jones farm exactly as indicated on Angela's map. The farm house was a large ranch style house with red brown trim. Two large Sego palms flanked the walkway to the house. A vegetable garden could be seen in back. A barn housing large farm equipment sat behind an asphalt parking area. The place looked clean and prosperous. Daphne was still taking in the scenery as Emma walked determinedly toward the door. Daphne hurried after her.

Matilda Jones answered the door after the first knock. She had obviously been watching them come up the drive. "You must be Ms. Anderson. I'm glad you called before you came. It's a long drive out here if no one's home." She motioned the women into the living room. "Have a seat. Can I offer you some decaf tea or lemonade? My doctor won't let me have caffeine anymore."

"Lemonade would be great." Emma answered for them both.

"Me too," echoed Daphne, feeling somewhat left out between waiting in the kitchen and having her order placed for her like she was a small child.

"Oh, I'm sorry. This is Daphne Armstrong, my legal secretary."

Daphne stood to shake hands with Matilda. "Nice to meet you."

"Nice to meet you," Daphne said as she shook hands with her hostess. "What a lovely home."

"Thank you. Are you from Houston?"

"Yes, my sons and I live near downtown."

"Oh, you have sons? How many?" Matilda asked, clearly pleased to find another mother she could tell about her children.

"Two, Jason who is thirteen and in the eighth grade and Gabe, my younger boy who just turned ten. Do you have a large family? I can see from the pictures you have some grandchildren?" Daphne turned the last statement into a question. Emma had been somewhat surprised to hear about her secretary's sons, but thought that she was certainly catching onto this small town approach.

"We have eight grandchildren, all younger than your boys," the retired nurse said with great pride. Matilda said, "They all moved away from Richmond, but they all live fairly close around here, so we get to see most of them every week. Well, let me get that lemonade. Y'all have a seat," she said as she stepped into the kitchen.

Once they were all seated with their lemonades, Emma began the conversation, "Do you still remember me? You worked for Daddy for so many years." Daphne cringed inwardly at Emma's overly direct approach. Clearly someone who offered you lemonade and sat you in the living room respected the social niceties.

"Sure, I remember when you weren't bigger than a minute," the older woman responded. "I haven't seen you since your father's funeral, but I've kept up with you, through the paper and around. Are you still in Houston?"

Emma was somewhat distracted that someone she had totally forgotten about would know about her life. She had momentarily forgotten what Richmond was like. Everyone knew about everyone else. She reminded herself that she better play the game, or she wouldn't get all the information she wanted. "Yes, Bill, my husband and I are still there. We both work for law firms. And how have you been? You really look good. You're still very trim. How do you avoid gaining weight?"

"You just don't eat too much." Matilda still told it like it was. "By the way, how's your mother?"

"She's not doing well," Emma answered. Of course, Matilda would know that. Emma wondered what she was getting at.

"I didn't think she'd live this long. Ed and I are members of the Baptist Church so I always looked on alcoholism as a personal weakness. Now some people say it's a disease. I always knew your mother had a drinking problem but neither Dr. Coleman nor I ever mentioned it."

"You always liked Dad didn't you?" Emma tried to take control of the conversation again.

"Doctor Coleman was the kindest, gentlest man I ever knew. There was never any romantic interest between us. I loved Ed, and the doctor was a straight arrow. I really respected the doctor."

Well, Daphne thought, *that about covers all the bases. This lady certainly puts all her cards on the table.*

Emma took a deep breath, sighed, and started to tell Matilda briefly more about what had happened. She had explained on the phone that she was representing some people with a claim against Zunker Chemical. Now she explained about the babies, saying "You remember Samuel Cox? He and his wife Ann had a deformed baby. The baby was early and didn't live. My son, David Jesse," Emma paused. She knew that Matilda would recognize her father's name. "He didn't live but a few minutes. Both these babies, and more, had rachischisis, you know where the spine doesn't close? Well, they have identified this as a chromosome thirteen problem. The only place that we can figure out we could have gotten this mutation is from the spill that Zunker had. That's why I need to look at Dad's medical records from the time of the spill out at the plant. Do you still have them?"

Matilda had listened quietly to Emma's explanation. Daphne couldn't tell if she was moved by the story, if she believed the story, or what. "Every one of them. I don't think there'd be any problem with letting you see them. I'd have to keep 'em here, but you could bring a copy machine out and make copies."

"Matilda, I love you!"

Back in the car, retracing their way back to the freeway and Houston, Emma was euphoric. "Thanks, this was a great idea. Now all we need to do is copy those files. I can't wait to see Mr. Jon Miller's face when he figures out that I got the information without his precious files."

They were flying down the back roads, but there was no traffic, so Daphne thought that she would just sit down, shut up, and listen. "Yeah, this will show him. I'm surprised that Matilda didn't say more about the problem, aren't you?"

"Oh, I bet she was just happy to get such good gossip to tell at the next meeting with her church ladies. That's why I didn't mention everyone. Only those who are open about their loss. Wasn't I clever to drop the baby's name? I knew she would recognize that I had used Dad's name."

"Yeah, that was good. Now all we have to do is find a copier to rent, buy some paper, and we're in business." Daphne was pretty clear who would run the copies, but still, Emma was on an upswing. Work was work, so who was she to complain?

After Daphne finished arranging for them to pick up the copier, a case of paper, and some toner in the morning, Emma said, "Call Bill and see where he takes the car. The check engine light came on, whatever that means. I think it has something to do with the pollution control system of the car. Anyhow it needs to go in for service."

Bill answered, clearly expecting Emma, but Daphne explained, "Bill, this is Daphne. Emma's car needs to go in for service. Where did you take it? What's the procedure, do I call for an appointment?"

Bill replied, "George is our service advisor. Let me get the number. He knows all about the car." It was clear he was somewhat disappointed that the call wasn't about the possibility of reconciliation he still expected. After giving her the number, he asked, "How is everything else?"

"About the same, thanks," was the best Daphne could manage

with Emma sitting right there. "O.K., I'll tell her you asked. And tell her to call you. Thanks, Bill."

"Guess you heard that?" she asked, as she started to dial the service advisor's number.

"Yeah, I'll call him in a few days, when I have something to tell him," Emma answered, clearly unconcerned.

"When do you want to take the car in?" she asked, while she waited to be connected to George.

"Anytime after tomorrow. Tomorrow is for the files." While her secretary made the appointment, Emma thought about her life, about what she was going to do after the lawsuit finished, and she had her divorce. Making partner was still one of her goals, she decided. No problem about the divorce, the firm would see it as a way for her to bill more hours, since she didn't have any family commitments. She would put the money from Hays aside for something special, maybe a beach house. She probably should think about what sort of divorce settlement she wanted. She was the only one who had any money of her own, since she had the money from her dad's estate. She had been very careful not to co-mingle it with hers and Bill's. No, that was clearly hers. Half of the money from the house, and then they would each just take their own 401K plans. Bill probably didn't want any of the furniture. They could each take a car. *It was going to be surprisingly easy,* she thought. *Several things to do, but none of them would be hard. And I can get Daphne to help with most of them.*

Emma and Daphne returned to the farm the next afternoon with a small portable copy machine and five reams of copy paper. Matilda led them to a small room off the barn. The charts were stored in four filing cabinets in the same room. Matilda was short and wore her grey hair up in a bun. With charts piled on the filing cabinets, often all you could see was the bun bobbing up and down over the top of the charts. The filing was precise, just as you would have expected from a bright, hard-working nurse.

"They're filed alphabetically. The date of the last time they were seen is the last date posted on the side of the jacket. If you need x-rays, I have them in the next room in the large wooden files. Laboratory data is filed in the chart. I'll just watch you examine the first few files. I'll re-file them. I don't think you'll need any help reading the doctor's handwriting. If you do, I'll be in the kitchen."

"Let's see if we can find the charts on the people who worked at the plant. You take half the list; I'll take the other." Jon's list of employees had come in handy after all.

Within an hour they had located all the charts corresponding to the employee list from Hays Chemical, including Henderson W. Williams. After Matilda saw that Daphne treated the files with care, stacking them in alphabetical order, she left quietly. One after another in her father's neat, engineering like script, the charts began, "This is a xx year old employee of Zunker Chemical Plant in Thompsons, Texas, who allegedly was exposed to the neurotoxic material produced at the plant during a chemical spill last week. According to the history given, cattle on lands surrounding the plant were killed. They have been sent to A&M for autopsy. The name of the toxic substance is unknown to the patient. By history given it can cause respiratory collapse and death. It may also be mutagenic." None of the patients showed any physical or laboratory abnormalities related to the toxin.

"Hot damn!" cried Emma. "We've got the motherfuckers by the balls now!"

Daphne grinned, "It ain't gonna be pretty!" *Good that Matilda didn't hear that,* she thought. *It would blow the tiny bit of sympathy that she has for our case.*

When they had finished making copies, Daphne suggested that Emma tell Matilda that they were ready to re-file everything.

"Thank you, Matilda. We've got what we needed. You might be called as a witness, but the files were the main thing," Emma said as Daphne loaded the car.

"We left the files on top of the cabinet, like you asked," Daphne explained. "I don't think that we messed anything up. Thanks again for letting us do this."

"Glad they could help. That's what Dr. Coleman wanted, why he set up the fund, so that people could get what they needed from the files. I guess you'll let me know if you need me to testify?" she asked.

"Yes, you would get a subpoena, that's how it's done. It won't mean that you've done anything wrong. I'll call you if it looks like that is happening."

Daphne made a mental note to remember to call Matilda if subpoenas were being issued. She wasn't sure why, but she didn't think Matilda was as much on Emma's side as Emma did.

The next afternoon, Emma came back from meeting with the realtor about showing the house. "Daphne, that woman Silvia is a mover and a shaker. She's already setup a showing for this Sunday afternoon. The signs just went up, and she's already had three calls. Says she thinks she can get full asking price.

"But back to the case at hand, have you prepared all the chart copies? I need one copy for Judge Carlson and one for Jon Miller, representing Hays Chemical."

"Yes. They're over there on your desk in two manila envelopes labeled Hays and Miller. What do you think your chances of getting them admitted are?" Daphne asked.

"We'll see tomorrow. We meet with Carlson and Miller at ten in the judge's chambers. Guess we need to leave here about half past eight, don't you think?"

"Sounds about right to me," Daphne answered, but Emma had already gone into another part of the apartment.

The next morning when Daphne came to work, Emma handed her a list of three divorce attorneys and their contact information on a sheet of paper. "No sense in putting this off any longer. Check these guys out; find out how much of a retainer each charges, how many hours they would estimate for an uncontested divorce, no children, but some property. I did a pretty good job of keeping things separate, but we will have to do some sort of property settlement," Emma told

Daphne, but she was speaking mostly to herself. "Of course I want all the work done by the man on the list; I don't want to get handed off to some newbie attorney," she continued. By this point Daphne had begun making notes.

"See which one you can get the first appointment with. You may have to make appointments with several, then cancel any that don't work. I'll be back in a few hours, and we can see where you are. Mostly what I want to know is what the timeline looks like.

"The realtor seems to be working out well. She thinks she has someone interested in the house. Says I should see the first offer in a day or two." Emma was gathering her purse and briefcase, clearly on her way out of the office.

"Oh, you better check with Bill on those attorneys. You have his office number, don't you?" When Daphne nodded, too stunned to speak, Emma continued, "Make sure he hasn't already retained one of them. Then check that he doesn't have any conflict with them. Check with them that they don't have some relationship with Bill. Bill went to Rice, played baseball. Just make sure they don't have any conflict representing me against Bill. This might get him off high center. I'm sure he hasn't done anything yet."

Daphne found her voice, "Should I remind him of the offer on the house? Let him know the offer might be coming?"

"You could tell him about it. That's a good idea. He knows the house is on the market. I told him I was going to put the house up for sale." Emma thought back to the last time they had seen each other. She told him she was going to "sell the fucking house," so he should have figured it out from that.

Bill left a message on her cell phone every couple of days, asking how she was, inquiring about progress on the case. Emma never answered when she saw it was Bill. She had left a couple of return messages on his work phone, late at night when she knew he wouldn't be there. He still had his office with all that support. He should be getting the divorce attorneys and selling the house. Here she was, as usual, doing all the work.

"You better run the list of names by him first. Then tell him about the house. If I like the offer, or when we get to an offer I like," Emma amended, "we'll send it over for him to sign. I'll be back in a couple of hours. I've got to get ready for tomorrow."

Daphne had been making some notes as Emma spoke, but she looked up as Emma left. This certainly wasn't the first time she had been asked to make personal appointments. Attorneys in the firm were busy, worked long hours, but this was the first time she had even heard of someone's secretary getting a divorce for them, even for a partner, and they did almost nothing for themselves.

Oh well, she thought, picking up the phone to call Bill, *I had always thought that the reason Emma hadn't had me pick up things at the cleaners was that they were delivered to her house. Now,* she revised her concept, *I guess maybe ol' Bill picked up the cleaning.* Daphne punched in the numbers for Bill's office.

It was early afternoon when Emma returned. As Daphne suspected, she had a new hair trim and a fresh manicure. Whatever made her feel good and helped her do her best in court tomorrow was O.K. with Daphne.

"How did it go?" she asked flipping through the mail that Daphne had put on her desk. "Did I get a fax from the realtor?"

"Nothing from the realtor." After her emotional call with Bill, Daphne had worried about how to tell her boss about the call, about how Bill was doing. Then, over her sandwich in the apartment kitchen at lunch, it dawned on her that Emma didn't want to hear about Bill's shock or even his tears. She probably didn't even care. She only wanted the information that affected her. So that's what Daphne would tell her: information.

"Bill hadn't realized you were as far along on selling the house. I think he'll sign any offer you send him when you get one.

"As far as the divorce attorneys, he hadn't retained one yet. He understands that he needs to. And the second one on the list, James Woodson, he has played golf with him a couple of times. No conflict, but that's the only one he knew." Damn, a couple of sentences to summarize the worst conversation in her life including when she had told her mother she was leaving the no-good SOB who was the father of her sons (and who knows how many others). No mention of Bill's begging her to talk to Emma—talk her out of doing this, to get Emma to see him, just for a few minutes. Poor bastard thought he could convince his wife to try again, at the marriage, at everything.

Daphne had finally said she would talk to Emma. And she was, wasn't she? It didn't help her conscience much, but she had had to get that begging, weeping man off the phone.

"With the divorce attorneys, I called the first one and got some run around. They suggested you would want to call. So, for the third one, I skipped the second one, I said it was for a client of yours. That you needed to know how much, how soon, and if there was anything to hurry the process."

"Good idea. You're catching on."

Daphne wasn't sure that coming up with a lie that Emma approved of was a good thing. She handed Emma the figures. It looked like six months at least, but Emma didn't seem to be in a terrible hurry to be divorced. She didn't think Emma had anyone waiting in the wings. She only seemed to want to get the ball rolling. Or maybe it was just tasks to keep her secretary busy, and now was as good a time as any. Daphne couldn't be sure.

"All right Ms. Anderson, what have we here?" asked Judge Carlson, glancing at the two attorneys.

Emma replied, "When your honor denied my request for access to the Zunker records, you told me that I'd have to find another source for my information about toxic products from Zunker Chemical. These papers indicate that I found another source. Rather than argue this out in open court, I thought I'd bring this up in chambers to see about admissibility. These are copies of charts from my father's patient records. My father was Dr. Jess Coleman. He saw all of the Zunker employees at this plant after the alleged spill.

These records confirm the exposure. And they describe the product as mutagenic."

"Well, it looks like you found another source. Mr. Miller, what are your thoughts on these?"

"How are you going to document authenticity of the records? For all we know these could be made up." Jon was reaching, but he had to put up some fight. The records couldn't say that the chemical had caused the mutation, but it would be better if they were excluded.

"I will depose Matilda Jones, my father's long-time nurse, who has been custodian of these documents. She will swear to the validity of these documents." Emma expected to have to authenticate them, which should be a snap; Matilda had barely allowed them to copy the charts. Her father had certainly chosen a conscientious guardian for his records.

"Your honor," said Jon, "I have no objection provided I have the ability to cross examine Ms. Jones and provided I am given opportunity to examine all the charts of Dr. Coleman in their entirety and in their original form."

"What say you, Ms. Anderson?"

Emma hadn't expected the request for the entire file. She didn't know what Jon hoped to learn. Maybe he was simply being difficult. "I don't know why you won't settle for the photocopies if we authenticate them."

"That's my offer, take it or leave it. We can always argue it out in open court."

"O.K., I accept," Emma answered. "Your honor, I will need a court order from you to allow Matilda Jones to bring all the files to a deposition and allow Mr. Miller to examine them," she was resigned. She hadn't won every skirmish, quite the opposite. Finding the charts had been her only win, but she was determined it would be enough to win the war.

"I know Matilda. We went to high school together. It may take more than a court order, but we'll start there. Pick it up from my clerk in a couple of days." Judge Carlson said, "I'm so glad you children are learning to play nice. Ms. Anderson, please make all the charts in their entirety available to Mr. Miller at least two days prior to your deposing Ms. Jones. Anything else? No? Carry on then." He stood and both attorneys followed him out.

When she got back to Houston, Emma summarized the morning's events, "Daphne, I've had a good day. Judge Carlson may not be such a bad egg . . . and Jon was certainly fair . . . demanding but fair. We can admit the charts, but ol' Jon gets to look at all of 'em beforehand. Maybe we can learn to play nicely, and maybe they'll make a settlement offer after the depositions."

"I'd certainly like to play nicely with ol' Jon-boy. That man has got a body and a smile that does things," she teased. It was good to see her boss relaxing a bit. She had certainly been wound up tight the past few months.

"You know, Daphne, I'm not really in this for the money. I just want to rub the bastards' noses in it. But if we do get some money, I don't want Bill to get his hands on any of it. He really had no part in all this except providing a defective sperm . . . and he enjoyed doing that," Emma continued, thinking out loud.

"We've got to make sure that the divorce takes place before any settlement comes from the chemical company. I'll call that attorney you found and get things rolling. Do you have his name? You know the one who said he could usually get an uncontested case through in six months?"

"Oh yeah, James Woodson, I have his number right here." Daphne had learned to keep all her notes with her. Emma was always asking for a name or a phone number. She reached into the drawer for the folder that she had labeled "Anderson v. Anderson." It seemed kinda brutal, but she couldn't think of anything else to call it.

"Give him a call. See if you can get me in tomorrow or even the next day. Tomorrow is better. You know money isn't enough for all the shit I had to go through, but a green poultice would help."

CHAPTER 15

Jon and Cato preferred to run in the early morning, but at times, depending on court schedules, afternoon runs were necessary. In the afternoon, Jon kept Cato on a long rope leash, but in the early mornings when the town was still asleep, Cato could run free.

So when Jon came home in the late afternoon and got out the rope leash, Cato would come and nuzzle Jon, making it difficult to put on the rope. Eventually they made it to the street. They ran down the oak-lined streets of old Richmond. Only an occasional car was seen.

They came down Main Street in front of the Jane Long Elementary School. The school had just celebrated its one hundredth anniversary. Most of the long-time residents of Richmond had been students in this school and had fond memories of their school days.

A group of six boys played three-on-three basketball on an asphalt court behind the main building. The squads had obviously been chosen on the basis of friendship and not on the basis of height. Three tall "skins" were teamed against three short "shirts." Cato had decided to "mark his territory" at the base of a tall cottonwood tree. Jon stopped to watch the game.

The three "skins" were much slower than their shorter opponents but with their superior height were able to block many of the shots by the "shirts." With faster feet and quicker hands, the "shirts" made frequent steals. Jon watched for about ten minutes with neither side making a basket. Finally one boy on the "skins" lost a shoe; time was called while he re-tied his Nike. Jon asked, "What's the score?" "Two to two," said the shortest "shirt" as the game resumed.

Jon mused, *A good defense is not enough. You have to score points to win. My defense against Mrs. Anderson has been good, but I need to score points if I want to win.*

"Ms. Anderson, Jon Miller here. I have my list of witnesses that I'd like to depose in the Hays case. Unless your appeals are successful, I won't depose anyone one from Homeland Security, Defense, or Environmental Protection. If your appeals were to be successful, I'd like to reserve the right to add those names."

"Sounds reasonable to me, Jon."

"Where do you want me to have the court send the list?" he asked.

"I've filed my address with the court," she replied, not wishing to let him know she was working in a rented apartment.

"Ms. Anderson, could we agree to only list those we really intend to depose? I know a lot of large Houston firms list everybody and his dog, attempting to swamp a 'poor' one man show with hundreds of names that one man can't possibly research." *Might as well try to get a level playing field,* thought Jon.

"That'll be fine," said Emma, not wanting to admit that she was a one woman firm, and no more eager to wade through a long list than Jon was. "We could, perhaps, agree by mutual consent to allow additional names if needed." No need to tell him that she hadn't yet found a toxicologist who would say any unnamed substance could cause mutations.

"That'll be fine with me. I'll fax my list to the clerk of the court. Would you send me a copy of your list to the office either by fax or 'snail mail?'"

"Maureen, would you please make a list of witnesses for deposition in the Hays case? List Loretta Ann Boone and Dr. Arthur

Bardwil Richter. Don't list any addresses. Make her search for them. A smart, big-city attorney should have no trouble with that."

Dr. Singh walked into the office of Ralph Reynolds, chair of the department of Developmental Medicine at Baylor University College of Medicine. A worried frown dominated Singh's usually cheerful face.

"Raj, what's the matter? You look like somebody pissed in your Wheaties." Dr. Reynolds was known for his "plain speaking."

"I am very concerned. This woman who helped me with my statistics has now called me and told me I must testify in a lawsuit she is bringing, not against me or us. Against Hays Chemical Company. Today I received these papers . . . a subpoena. I have to give a deposition. I do not understand the workings of the American judicial system or any other judicial system. I do not know if I am in trouble."

"Tell me the whole story. Begin at the beginning," Ralph told him with a sympathetic look on his face. "And calm down, sit down, and tell me."

Raj began at the beginning, recounting Emma's entire story. Ralph listened intently.

"Raj, do you think she got the names of other couples from your registry? That's the only thing I could think of that might get you in trouble."

"I don't know. I just don't know," he was almost whining, his anxiety was so great.

"Most of the practicing physicians have been involved in malpractices cases. I've given depositions in those before. Even testified. Look, if it'll make you feel any better, we can call Wayne Alcorn, the school attorney and let him look into it. He is very knowledgeable about this sort of thing."

"I would appreciate it, very much," he answered, somewhat calmer.

"Let's do it right now."

Ralph twirled the Rolodex on his desk. He dialed the four-digit extension. The phone was picked up on the first ring, "Office of Wayne Alcorn. Mary Lou speaking. How may I help you?"

"This is Doctor Reynolds, chair of Developmental Medicine. May I speak to Mr. Alcorn?"

"Just a moment."

"Wayne Alcorn here," came the prompt greeting.

"Hey, Wayne, this is Ralph Reynolds in Developmental Medicine. One of my boys over here just received a subpoena for a deposition in a civil suit. He's not a party to the suit, but he's got some concerns. Can he come over and talk to you about this? Right now all his sphincters are puckered and until we can get them to relax, I'm not going to get any work out of him," he smiled over at Raj.

"You have the quaintest way of expressing yourself. Send him on over and tell him to bring the subpoena with him."

"Raj, take your subpoena, and get your butt over to Alcorn's office. It's room one twelve in the DeBakey Building. And quit worrying . . .they serve good food in American prisons." He laughed and stood as the younger man left.

Dr. Singh didn't have any trouble finding the attorney's office. As soon as he stepped into the secretary's outer office, Wayne said, "Come in Dr. Singh. Tell me what's going on, and let me see your subpoena." He took the subpoena and then shook Raj's hand. "Have a seat. Can I get you a Coke, coffee, water?"

"No, thank you," murmured Raj, the frown still dominating his face. After the attorney read the subpoena, he prompted the doctor to tell him all he knew about Emma and her problems.

Alcorn looked at the subpoena again and said, "Let me call this Emma Anderson and see what's going on."

Mr. Alcorn quickly dialed the number listed on the subpoena. After three rings, Daphne picked up, "Law office of Emma Anderson, Daphne Armstrong speaking. How may I help you?"

"This is Wayne Alcorn, attorney for Baylor University College of Medicine. One of our faculty just received a subpoena from Mrs.

Anderson. I wanted to speak to her about this to find out what was going on."

"Mrs. Anderson isn't here at the moment. I'm her legal assistant. We want to have Dr. Singh testify about his research on chromosome thirteen and neural tube closure. We have three clients at the present time who had affected babies. Dr. Singh is the world's leading authority on this. I tried to explain to him in a phone call yesterday that he would receive the subpoena and that we would compensate him for his time . . . one hundred and fifty dollars per hour for preparation and travel time and three hundred dollars an hour for time in the deposition. We didn't think that we needed to discuss his testimony with him because the questions are all very basic. I guess that I didn't make myself clear. What concerns does he have?" Daphne had gone through the procedure with Singh, but even during the call she had sensed that he was extremely uncomfortable. She had expected something like this.

"No concerns, we just require our faculty to present any subpoenas for review. Can't be too careful these days. Thank you very much. I don't need to speak to Ms. Anderson. You've answered my questions."

"Goodbye."

"Dr. Singh, you have nothing to worry about. They are just using you to provide background information. They will ask general questions well within your ability to answer. If it is a question you can't answer, you simply say that is not your area of expertise. You're not in any trouble," he explained.

"I'm still quite concerned. I know so little about the judicial system in America."

"Look if it will make you feel any better, I'll make up some practice questions and we can go over them together. I'll go with you to the deposition to make sure things go smoothly. I'll send the questions over tomorrow. You look them over, and then we'll set up a time to go over them together. Call me after you have a chance to look over the questions. And smile, things are O.K." The attorney was actually pleased to have a faculty member come with a problem he could solve and a subpoena that didn't put millions of dollars from the medical school at risk and involve lots of T.V. cameras. This case would be a piece of cake, and he would get out of the office for a while.

A glimmer of a smile crossed Raj's face. "Thank you. I'll call you as soon as I see the questions."

CHAPTER 16

O.K., folks, we're going live. This is the video-taped deposition of Raj Singh in the law offices of Jonathon Miller." The video tech then turned on the lights and video camera. "This is Jerome Johnson, court reporter. Dr. Singh, do you swear that the testimony you are about to give in the matter now pending will be the truth, the whole truth and nothing but the truth?"

"I do." Raj Singh sat at the end of the conference table opposite the camera with his attorney, Wayne Alcorn, at his side. Before the recording session had begun, Emma had tried to understand why Dr. Singh had an attorney with him. In response to her question, Dr. Singh only replied, "My employer agrees with me. One cannot be too cautious when it comes to lawsuits."

Emma wondered, *Was it seeing my name on the subpoena or had there been other suits about the rachischisis?* She wouldn't learn any more from him, but she could always call the technician, whatever her name was, to find out about the climate in the lab. Or, had the list of plaintiffs on the suit clicked with him as being the patients in his files? Maybe he wasn't quite as slow as she had thought.

Emma sat on one side of the table and Jon Miller on the other. All of the principles had a microphone in front of them. Daphne was sitting at the back of the room, and Maureen had been in and out of the room several times helping get everything set up.

Emma began, "First I want to thank Mr. Miller for the use of his conference room. Good morning, Dr. Singh. As you know I'm Emma Anderson, attorney and principle, in a suit against Hays Chemical, represented by Mr. Jonathon Miller, who sits across the table from me. Have you ever given a deposition before Dr. Singh?"

"No, I have not." He glanced at his attorney nervously.

"Then I'll go over some of the rules of the game: You are under oath to tell the truth. An untruth is perjury and may be punished by fine and/or imprisonment. Please let me finish my question before you attempt to answer. Speak loudly and as clearly as possible. Nodding your head is not an acceptable way to answer a question. Please say 'Yes' or 'No' and not 'Uh huh' or 'Unh huh.' If you don't understand a question, please ask me to repeat it or re-phrase it. Please don't guess at answers. If you don't know, just say so. Any questions?"

"No." Both Emma and Jon noticed that the witness had glanced at his attorney before answering even this innocuous question.

"Please state your full name and your address," Emma continued.

"Rajmada Maharashrta Singh, five fifty-five Holly Street, Bellaire, Texas."

"What is your occupation?" Again he looked at his attorney, but this time it was only a glance.

"I am assistant professor of medicine at Baylor College of Medicine in Houston, Texas. I am in the section of developmental medicine. I also conduct research funded by the National Institutes of Health."

"Are you a U.S. citizen?" Jon glanced at Emma. Where was she going with this? He noticed that this line of questioning caused an exchange of glances between Singh and his attorney. Jon smiled to himself at the somewhat comic nature the deposition was taking on.

"Yes. I was born in New York State. My parents are naturalized citizens. Both were born in India."

"Tell us about your educational qualifications."

"I attended private schools through high school, all in New York State. I received my undergraduate degree in Biochemistry and Genetics at New York University, where my parents are on the faculty. I received my Masters Degree and Ph.D. from Stanford.

After my graduation I joined the faculty at Baylor." He seemed to be calming down as the questioning continued.

"Do you have an area of special interest in your research, Dr. Singh?" Emma asked.

"Yes. My current area of special interest is in the role of chromosome thirteen in fusion of the neural tube in fetal development." Despite her 'rules of the game' preface, Emma was somewhat surprised at the extremely specific response. Clearly Dr. Singh had been well prepared for this deposition.

"Could you explain that in terms a layman could understand?" she prompted.

"Yes, of course. The human fetus starts out as a union of a male sperm and a female egg. Genetic material is contributed by each parent. In the human there are twenty-three pairs of chromosomes. One part of each pair comes from the mother and one from the father. Each pair of chromosomes has a somewhat different appearance that allows them to be distinguished. The nervous system of a fetus starts out as a flat surface which forms two parallel ridges that ultimately fuse into what is called the neural tube. This becomes the brain and spinal cord. This development appears to be under the control of the chromosome given the number thirteen. I am studying this to see if I can find the location of this gene and to understand the enzymatic reactions that it governs." Dr. Singh watched Emma to see if his explanation was acceptable.

Evidentially it was, because she continued with the questioning, asking, "What does failure of fusion mean for the fetus?"

"There is a spectrum ranging from spina bifida to myelomeningocoel or meningocoel depending on the extent of the lack of fusion. Symptoms can range from none or minimal to a state incompatible with life. In this present case, none of the spine or brain fused. And none of the fetuses lived."

"What causes this?" At the crux of the case, Emma was brief and very pointed.

"No one knows. It is obviously genetic . . . an abnormality in chromosome number thirteen . . . but what causes the abnormality is not known. Speculation includes a spontaneous mutation occurring at a weak bond in the person's DNA, a virus altering the DNA, irradiation damage, or DNA damage due to toxic chemical exposure. At the present we do not know."

"What is a mutation, doctor? Again, in terms that a layman can understand, please."

"It is a rare, random, and inheritable change in a cell's genetic material . . . a change in the order of the chemicals, called base pairs, which make up the strands of DNA which make up the chromosomes. Since you have a pair of the DNA strands, changes in one strand may not bring about an identifiable change in a fetus on a gross level because the unchanged DNA takes over total function. We call this a recessive mutation. If the new DNA takes over function and brings about a change in the fetus we can identify, we call it a dominant mutation.

"If expression of a mutation can cause death of the fetus, it is called a lethal mutation. If this change is recessive it may be passed on, unexpressed, for generation after generation with no apparent effect on the individual. If, however, two individuals with the same recessive lethal mutation have children, they have a one-in-four chance that a fetus would receive two lethal recessives, one from each parent. That fetus will not be viable and should be terminated." Jon's head popped up from his note taking to stare first at the witness, then at Emma, and finally at the witness' attorney. Mr. Alcorn rolled his eyes when Jon looked at him.

"We were speaking in generalities, Dr. Singh, but let's be more specific. What is the cause of the fetal death in the three families in this particular case?"

"There is an abnormal chromosome thirteen in each of the parents. It represents a recessive lethal mutation."

"What caused these mutations, doctor?"

"I don't know." He looked straight at Emma first, then glanced at his attorney.

"Could exposure to toxic chemicals have caused this?"

"That has been suggested as a cause, but I do not know."

"I pass the witness." Emma turned to look at Jon.

"Hello. My name is Jon Miller, attorney for Hays Chemical. I don't believe we've met?" The slight inflection was the only indication of a question. Emma watched for the exchange of glances between her expert witness and his attorney, but saw nothing. Was the attorney to protect Singh from her, she wondered?

Possibly, because he answered Jon's implied question without hesitation, "No, I don't believe we've met before. How do you do?"

"Doctor, how common are lethal recessive genes in the population as a whole?"

"The average human carries three to five lethal recessive genes."

"With so many lethal recessives, why don't we see more of these disasters?"

"Our breeding population is so large that we don't often run into another person with the same lethal recessive."

"Doctor, I've often wondered about those Egyptian Pharaohs who had all those hundreds of children. I understand that brothers and sisters often married. Wouldn't that cause problems?"

"Theoretically, if a Pharaoh had a lethal recessive, one-half of his children would be carriers. If two of his children with recessive mutations married, statistically one-fourth of their children would be normal non-carriers, one-half would be carriers but appear normal, and one-fourth would die."

"One last question: Can you tell us what caused this mutation?"

"No, I cannot," Dr. Singh answered succinctly.

"Thank you, doctor."

The video tech shut down the equipment and prepared to go find some lunch. Emma and Jon agreed to meet back in the conference room in two hours. Emma and Daphne followed the video tech out, leaving Maureen and Jon in the conference room.

"Do you want me to run to the HEB and grab you a sandwich?" Maureen asked, knowing that Jon would spend his lunch break returning calls.

"Please, pick us both up something, if you don't mind," Jon answered and handed Maureen a twenty.

Jon went to his office and picked up the phone. Time to do some more research on his own approach, not just those blocking moves of Mrs. Anderson.

"Texas A&M School of Veterinary Medicine. How may I direct your call?"

"Hi. I'm Jon Miller, an attorney in Richmond, Texas. I represent Hays and Zunker Chemical Companies. About fifteen years ago, Hays sent a number of dead cattle killed after a chemical spill to be studied at A&M. The doctor's name on the correspondence I have was Talmadge Reese, D.V.M. Is he still there?"

"Yep, he's still alive and kicking. He's now chair of the department of pathology. I'll connect you. Have a good one."

"Department of Pathology. Office of the Chairman. Margaret Baker speaking. How may I help you?"

"My name is Jon Miller. I'm an attorney in Richmond, Texas. May I speak to Dr. Reese?"

"Just a moment."

"Dr. Reese here."

"Dr. Reese, I'm Jon Miller, an attorney in Richmond, Texas."

"We didn't do it and if we did, we didn't mean to and we're sorry. Seriously what can I do for you."

"I don't know if you remember but about fifteen years ago you did autopsies on cattle killed during a chemical spill at Zunker Chemical down south of Richmond. There would have been more than thirty of them. That many at once might jog your memory. Hays Chemical was also involved."

"Yeah, I remember. Bought a new pickup with the extra money I made from all the autopsies. Hays paid off like gangbusters."

"We've got a lawsuit down here alleging that the same spill caused mutations in a number of people. When these individuals married, they had horribly deformed, stillborn kids. Do you still have any tissue from those cattle, and if you do, could you examine it for chromosomal abnormalities?"

"I will have to check, but in general we never throw away anything. Give me a day or two, and I'll get back to you."

"Thanks, doc. Hays will reward you handsomely for your efforts no matter what they show. What kind of pickup are you looking at now?"

"Well, I've got my eye on this Dodge," he chuckled. "I'll call you back within two days."

As Jon got off the phone, Maureen was coming in the back door with the sandwiches.

"Let's go have a very girly lunch at Kathy's Korner, this little tea room downtown," Emma said. "It's kinda cute and has great food."

"Sounds good," Daphne answered getting in her boss's car. *Here I am riding around in a Mercedes, on my way to a tea room. I'm really moving up,* she thought. *Now, if Emma can really pull this off, that will be great.*

After they were seated and the iced tea served, Emma started the review of the morning. "Dr. Singh was something, wasn't he, with his own attorney?"

Daphne knew her role well—agree, keep everyone's spirits high, and keep track of the time so they got back on time. "What do you think that was all about? It reminded me of Tom Cruise and Cuba Gooding, Jr. in *Jerry Maguire.*"

Emma laughed, "It did. I don't know who thought that up, but I'm only paying for Singh's time. You told him about the rates when you contacted him, didn't you?"

"Sure did. He was pretty rattled by the whole concept. I'm not sure he'll even invoice you."

"Well, I'm not paying until he does. And I won't pay for more than two hours of research. Shouldn't really pay for any, but since it's gonna to be Hays' money what the heck. And, he did help the case or at least his records did, so I guess I owe him something."

The waiter took their orders—Daphne went with the chicken

salad sandwich on a croissant and Emma had a salad that the waiter said was really large. After he left, Daphne asked, "Who is up this afternoon?" even though she had made the arrangements for Matilda Jones' appearance.

"Matilda Jones and her original, complete charts. I still don't see what he's going to do with those. As soon as we establish that there was an exposure, and I find some old little league schedules, Hays will have to see the benefit of settling."

The waiter returned with their meals. Between bites, they agreed that the food was excellent, and even Emma acknowledged that the salad was very large. Emma picked up the conversation topic, "I guess I need to do some research on what the settlement should be. That will be a bit hard because most similar judgments or settlements are sealed. We know that there were three babies involved from this."

Daphne had finished her sandwich and now got out her notebook to capture Emma's thoughts. In a couple of days Emma would think that she had dictated the first draft of the settlement agreement, and Daphne would have to come up with something. Always best to jot down anything that could help.

"Does it matter that the other women have kids already?" she asked.

"No, but we might expand the list of claimants to include the Cox kids. We will have to come up with a figure for each baby. Call someone in the litigation group at the firm and find out the starting price of death of a child, loss of procreation ability, and then throw in some other things, like, oh, death of a middle-aged adult, death of a range cow, and death of a riding horse. That should cover it. Besides, no one will pick up on what's going on. This is between Hays and me."

Daphne wrote quickly. She already knew which secretary she would check with on these figures.

"Of course we'll do the accounting to get all our court costs. Work in my hours at four hundred dollars per hour for all the deposition time and court time. And the usual two hundred and fifty an hour for all this preparation time."

They both declined dessert. Emma took the bill.

"Guess we'd better head back," Emma said leaving cash to cover the bill.

The deposition of Matilda Jones, Doctor Coleman's long-time nurse, began early in the afternoon in the same circumstances as that for Dr. Singh except she came alone. No attorney.

Emma began the questioning with the usual instructions for depositions. Then she asked, "What is your full name, please?"

"Matilda Annie Coleman Jones."

"Are you related to my father? I mean, Dr. Coleman?" Emma asked, clearly disturbed by her witness' response.

"Not that we could ever figure out. It was my maiden name. I'm from west Texas, and he was from Missouri. I don't think I was related to Dr. Coleman. But it is my name."

"What is your profession?" Emma asked somewhat sharply, peeved with herself for making such a simple mistake. She knew never to ask a question that she didn't know the answer to. And, unlike Dr. Singh's attorney, she obviously hadn't spent enough time preparing her witness.

"I am a registered nurse. I have been retired about a year."

"Where have you worked?"

"After getting my training at the University of Texas Medical Branch in Galveston, I came to work as a floor nurse at Polly Ryon Hospital in Richmond. I worked there for five and a half years. Then I worked for Dr. Jess Coleman in his clinic until he died – almost thirty years. I then returned to Polly Ryon as supervisor until I retired about a year ago. Now I'm a housewife and grandmother."

"Did Dr. Coleman ask you to do anything should he die or become incapacitated?"

"Yes, he asked me to be in charge of his patient records. His wife was in no condition to handle that job. His daughter had left to go to college, and he didn't want to burden her. I was paid from a trust he had set up, and I was to keep the records for twenty years. The first couple of years I had to send out a lot of copies of the records. The last few years I've had no call to get any records until this case came up."

"Have these records been in your possession since the doctor's death?"

"Yes."

"Now I want you to look at these charts I've pulled. These are the charts of the people who worked in the plant at Thompsons. Are these charts in the doctor's handwriting?"

"Yes."

"Pass the witness. Thank you, Ms. Jones."

"Is that all?"

"No, Ms. Jones. I'm Jon Miller, the attorney for Hays Chemical Company. I get to ask you a few questions, too. Have you given a deposition before?" Jon smiled at the older woman. And, to Emma's disgust, she smiled right back.

"No, sir, I haven't."

"You are doing very well. I have a few more questions, and we'll get you out of here. Thanks for coming in. Did you bring all the charts I asked you to?"

"Yes, they're over in that box," she said pointing to a copier paper box.

"Will you check with me on the names? Dr. Coleman delivered Bill and Emma Anderson, right?"

"Yes."

"Looks like he was the doctor for both of their parents . . . right? And also he was the doctor for Ann and Samuel Cox and their parents? And for Rachel Davis? What about their parents?

"Doctor Coleman had a huge practice including the parents of Bill Anderson. Doctor Coleman was Emma's father, you know. And he was the doctor for Samuel and Ann Cox. He was the doctor for Samuel's and Ann's mothers and Samuel's dad. Ann's dad went somewhere else. He was the doctor for Rachel Davis's parents. He delivered Rachel, Ann, and Samuel."

"Did he mention any abnormality in any of these people that might bear any relation to the present case?"

Emma spoke up, "Calls for a conclusion. I object."

Jon replied, "I think that an R.N. with well over thirty years experience is enough of an expert to answer this question. Ms. Jones, you may answer the question."

"No. They were all delightfully healthy."

"Was there any history in any of the charts suggesting exposure to toxic materials?"

"You mean of the people who worked in the plant or those families involved in this suit?"

"Just those families involving Emma and Bill Anderson, Rachel Davis, and Ann and Samuel Cox."

"No."

"On the charts of the patients working at the plant . . . did the doctor find any clinical evidence of exposure to toxic materials?"

"No."

"I have just a couple of more questions. I noticed a large red check mark on the front of many of the women's charts. What does that indicate?"

"That indicated that the woman got a special pelvic exam."

"What does that mean?" Jon asked.

"You know how some women hate pelvic exams . . . they say it's uncomfortable and embarrassing. Dr. Coleman would give the patient an I.V. injection of a short-acting barbiturate. It would put them to sleep for five to ten minutes, and he'd do the Pap smear and pelvic exam. The women loved it. He built up a huge practice on referral among women because of this," she explained, still somewhat in awe of the good doctor.

"Only one or two more. . ."

The door opened with a loud thud. Maureen ran into the conference room with an ashen face, "The police just called. Cato's been hit by a drunk driver . . . he's pretty bad off. No one knows how Cato got out, but the guy hit him and then hit a parked car. They've taken him to Doc Smalley's."

"Mrs. Anderson, Mrs. Jones . . . I know it's highly irregular but could we finish this some other day. My dog means a lot to me," Jon asked, visibly shaken. He was already gathering up his papers.

Emma said, "It's all right with me."

"I was leaving tonight to go to Beaumont to see my sister who is recovering from hip replacement. I was planning to stay about a week until her daughter can get down to stay with her," Matilda said.

Emma smiled, "You go on ahead, dear. You and Mr. Miller can finish up when you get back." *Couldn't hurt to try Jon's 'charm 'em' approach* she thought, *though she wasn't sure from the puzzled look Matilda gave her that it worked.*

"Thanks," yelled Jon over his shoulder as he bolted out the door.

Late that afternoon Jon got back to his office from the vet's where Cato was resting comfortably after surgery to set his broken leg. Jon started sorting through the papers on his desk and decided to report in to the Hays home office. The call went to Bob Duggan's voice mail. "This is Jon Miller in Richmond. Bob, this is just to let you know we've started the depositions in the Anderson suit. We're about half way through the witnesses. Her witnesses haven't added anything that I think Judge Carlson would see as substantial.

"I've been doing some independent research," he continued, "And those witnesses will appear next week. One of Mrs. Anderson's witnesses can't finish until the end of next week, so that's when we will resume the depositions.

"I'm guardedly optimistic," Jon concluded. "I'll have more for you in about three days. If you need me, you can reach me at my office." Jon left his number and hung up. A bit of a break, getting Bob's voice mail, he thought. He didn't need to give his theory out until he had some corroborating evidence. Next week would be soon enough.

"Man, you're early. How's Cato?" Maureen asked Jon.

"Fortunately it looked worse than it was. Doc Smalley did some nice needlepoint and he's gonna be fine. He'll stay at Doc Smalley's for about a week and will be back running in three or four weeks after that. He has a cast on the leg, but I'm not sure that will slow him down much." Jon had been more shaken by seeing Cato unconscious on the exam table than he had been by anything in a long time.

"I'm certainly glad. You two are rather testy if you don't get your run in," she said in a knowing way.

"You always say that, but I don't think I'm testy. And Cato is just energetic," he explained.

"Uh huh," was her only response.

Jon pulled a hand-written sheet from his pocket. "Call Dr. Richter over at the lab. I need these results yesterday. Make sure he gets consent forms. And have him pick up this book. Tell him to get the samples off the envelopes. If he has any questions have him call me." He headed into his office to see if Bob had called back. He would tell him about everything that had happened, but it was too soon to share his thoughts. There would be time enough for that when he had Dr. Richter's results, if they bore out his theory.

"The AC is on the fritz again. What do you want me to do?" she asked from his door. She was going to get through her list of questions before she let Jon out of her sight.

"Call the dealer and have him replace the damn unit with a new one. And get a five ton unit instead of a three . . . wait make it two threes. That way if one goes out we'll still have some AC. I want to be able to hang meat in here."

"Have you checked the bank balance lately? That's gonna be pretty expensive. Do you want a quote first?" Jon could always count on her to be practical, thorough, but very practical.

"I think I will have a big check coming in from Hays. They pay very promptly if you win." He should wait until he had the results of Richter's tests, but he was pretty sure his theory was right. He just needed to figure out how to get the evidence out in a way that would convince Mrs. Anderson and have her eager to sign a settlement holding Hays harmless. His work was sure cut out for him.

CHAPTER 17

Mrs. Anderson, this is Jon Miller, I know that we've got the tail-end of the Jones deposition. That won't take me more than fifteen minutes. Since we have the court reporter and all the T.V. jazz, could we do two quickies of mine? One is the librarian from the Albert library. I want her to authenticate the ownership of some items in the library. The second is my genetics expert. Basically, I want him to see you in action before the trial. I find it helpful for my witnesses to see the opposing attorney before the big show. All together it shouldn't take more than forty-five minutes." Jon had worked the librarian in neatly, hoping to minimize her importance.

"Sounds reasonable to me, Jon. Tomorrow at two at your office, right?" Emma answered with no additional questions or concerns about the witness list.

"Right." *Keep it short and sweet,* Jon thought as he hung up. His theory was coming together, but until he got some facts from these witnesses, a theory was all it was.

After the preliminaries and the re-swearing in, Jon asked, "Mrs. Jones, glad to see you again. I appreciate your coming back. Cato, my dog, is doing well. How is your sister?"

"She's doing as well as can be expected. Her daughter's with her now, and they get along really well," she replied.

"When we stopped last time, you had just told us that the red check mark on the chart jacket meant that the woman had gotten a special pelvic exam. Would you please go through a special pelvic exam step by step so that we can understand exactly what occurred?" Jon asked.

"Well, Dr. Coleman would start a saline I.V. in the patient's hand or arm. He used the tiniest butterfly needle, and he was very good. I never saw him miss on the first attempt. So they didn't even complain about getting stuck. He would have them on the exam table with their feet in the stirrups. They would be draped. He would give them an I.V. injection of a short-acting barbiturate. They would go to sleep, and Dr. Coleman would do the pelvic exam and Pap smear. These were women who for one reason or another dreaded the pelvic. The doctor was very fast, and he would be finished before they woke up about eight or ten minutes later. If he needed more time he injected a second dose if they started waking up. Most of the ladies never even realized that they had been asleep."

"Was Doctor Coleman ever alone with the women during the exam?"

"No. He was a stickler about that. He always had me in the room," Matilda answered confidently.

"What happened then?" Jon prompted.

"I'd run the sample up to the Path lab; it was one floor up. Dr. Coleman always made me check the specimen in myself after one time the path lab mixed up patients, and we got the wrong results."

"Were the women still asleep when you took the specimen to the lab?" Jon probed.

"Usually." The nurse was unclear about where the attorney was going with these questions.

"Did anything unusual ever happen during any of these exams?"

"No . . . well only once. The path lab was closed, and so I hurried right back. Dr. Coleman was tucking in his shirt and zipping up his pants when I came back in. He got real embarrassed. I told him, 'Don't worry, I've seen a man tuck in his shirt before.' We both laughed." She smiled at the memory.

"I pass the witness," Jon said. He sat down quickly, avoiding Emma's questioning look.

Emma said, "I have nothing more."

Within five minutes Mrs. Jones was gone, and Ms. Loretta Boone was in the witness chair.

After the usual preliminaries, Jon began, "Ms. Boone, what is your full name and what do you do?"

"My name is Loretta Ann Eisman Boone. I'm head librarian at the Albert Library in Richmond."

"Have you been at the library long?" Emma was amused to notice that Jon was more direct and business-like with this witness.

"About seventeen years."

"Were you at the library when Dr. Coleman's first day cover collection was given to the library?" Jon asked.

"Yes."

The witness didn't seem surprised at the question, but Emma wondered what was going on. This line of questioning didn't seem to have anything to do with Hays, Zunker, or the case actually. *Well,* she thought, *she would give Jon a bit longer, since she would get all her court costs back in the settlement anyway. It was Hays money that he was wasting.* As she half listened to the librarian, Emma looked over at Daphne who was listening intently. *Funny how routine depositions could become,* she thought. *This must be one of the few that Daphne has heard.*

"Do you know what his procedure was with his collection?"

"Yes." Again the answer was concise.

"Could you describe it for us?" Jon asked. He was expecting an objection to the hearsay nature of the testimony, but one never came.

"Each year he'd get a list of the dates and locations of the first day of issue from the U.S. Postal Service. Then he'd send a letter to the Postmaster in that town. He'd insert a self-addressed envelope inside the envelope that he'd send to the Postmaster. He'd ask the Postmaster to affix the new stamp on his self-addressed envelope, put on the first day cancel, and mail the letter back to him. He would have included a money order to cover the cost of the stamp."

"Was there anything in the self-addressed envelope that came back to him?"

"Yes. He always enclosed a note to himself. He'd put the note in the envelope, lick the envelope, and seal it tight. It was important for him to be able to say that his genuine first day cover had actually carried mail," she finished with some satisfaction.

"Now, Ms. Boone, does this album contain the envelopes of Dr. Coleman's first day covers created and handled exactly as you described?" Jon said and again sat down quickly.

"Yes."

"Did you see Dr. Arthur Richter obtain samples from these envelopes?"

"Yes."

"I pass the witness," Jon said and again sat down quickly.

It took a minute for his last comment to register with her. Emma had a puzzled frown on her face. "I have no questions." She glanced back at Daphne who shrugged. Emma had no idea where Jon was headed. Not a good spot for an attorney.

"Thank you, Ms. Boone," Jon said.

"Yes, of course. That was easy enough."

Again within five minutes, Ms. Boone had been replaced by Dr. Arthur Richter. After the usual preliminaries, Jon began his questioning, "What is your full name, and what do you do?" Dr. Richter was a scholarly looking man with a full beard. He had rimless glasses which he kept adjusting as he talked. He wore a blue bow tie . . . a real tie, not a clip-on, with his dark blue Brooks Brother's suit. In deference to the heat, he had left the vest at home.

"My full name is Arthur Bardwil Richter, and I'm president and founder of Scientific Forensic Laboratories of Houston. My company is an accredited forensic laboratory that performs many types of forensic analysis. We work for both defendants and law enforcement agencies. Most defendants want independent confirmation of police findings. And many smaller police agencies cannot afford to have the specialized equipment necessary for tests that they may need only once or twice a year." Obviously this was not this witness's first deposition.

Emma stared at this witness. A forensic expert. Was his plan to say that they didn't have the chromosome abnormality? To discredit

Singh's testing? Her mind raced as she paid careful attention to the questions. While she was able to follow the answers, she was not able to see where the answers led.

"What are your qualifications for this position?" Jon asked.

"I received a Bachelor's Degree in biology from Texas A&M University. I received an M.D., degree from the University of Texas Southwestern Medical School in Dallas. I did a one-year straight pathology internship at Parkland Hospital in Dallas. I did a Pathology residency at the Massachusetts General Hospital. I did a two-year fellowship in forensic pathology at Johns Hopkins in Baltimore. I went to work for the F.B.I. in their central laboratory. After five years, I was made chief of that section. I left the Bureau after seven more years because of the health of my mother. I returned to Houston so that my wife and I could take care of her. I set up my laboratory at that time. It is fully accredited."

Daphne could tell by the look on Emma's face that this witness was a surprise. *Surely Jon must have cleared him with her,* she thought. *I don't think Dr. Richter was on the original list.* She had that sinking feeling you get as the roller coaster tops the first incline, and you start the plunge. Why wasn't Emma objecting or asking for a break or something?

"Did you take DNA samples from various individuals and do you have the results for us?"

"Yes.

"I have all the paper work with consent forms there on the table."

Emma rose and said, "Could I have a moment to review the consent forms?" It wasn't much but it was all she could think of.

"Certainly," Jon responded, handing her the envelope.

She glanced at the forms. Standard consent for testing, and everything seemed to be in order. Not much to work with here. "Continue," she said and resumed her seat.

"I took buccal swabs from Ann and Samuel Cox."

Jon interrupted to ask "Buccal smears are where they rub a cotton swab inside your cheek, right?"

"That's correct. I took a buccal swab from Ann's mother and father. Samuel's mother is dead, but we were able to get DNA from her old hairbrush. Samuel's father is also dead, but we got a DNA sample from a stamp off a letter he wrote to Ann's mother. We got buccal smears from Rachel Davis and Ernie Schulze and from each of their parents."

Emma realized that Jon must have done some research, too, since she had left Ernie's name out of the suit. She could just picture Jon charming his way into Rachel Davis' confidence. *Bet she didn't hang up on him*, Emma thought sourly.

"We used the DNA samples that Emma and Bill Anderson had given to Dr. Singh's lab. We obtained buccal smears from both of Bill's parents. Mrs. Coleman gave us a buccal smear specimen although I don't think I could really get informed consent from her, but she did sign the form."

Daphne gave a soft gasp. "Finally, I got a DNA specimen for Dr. Coleman from the envelopes from his first day collection. I analyzed all of the specimens."

That's what the librarian was for, Emma realized.

"What are your conclusions?" Jon asked softly.

"Based on our DNA analysis and with a reliability such that there is less than one chance in a billion that our results are incorrect, we can say that Bill, Emma, Ann, Samuel, Rachel, and Ernie all have the same father . . . Dr. Jess Coleman. He is the source of the abnormal chromosome thirteen in all these individuals."

Jon had just begun to say, "I pass the witness," when he heard a loud thud.

Emma had fainted, and her head hit the table.

They placed her on the floor and placed wet compresses on her forehead. When she came to and was able to talk, Jon asked everyone to leave. Daphne didn't budge until Emma nodded to her slightly.

"Mrs. Anderson, I am willing to make you an offer. Withdraw your suit and declare Hays Chemical blameless. Evaluate all the possible victims of your father's patient rape. You can use the charts with the red checks to identify the people to study. Indemnify any of the people who have suffered financial loss. I don't care what story you tell them. We cannot let this happen again to innocent people. In return I promise never to disclose anything I have discovered about your father or any information about these people."

"It's a deal." Emma didn't have to think about it. For once Jon's being such an ethical bastard would work in her favor.

Jon heard Emma say to Daphne as her assistant helped her into the car, "At least I won't have to worry about getting a damn divorce. No way in fucking Hell I can be denied an annulment. I mean, I've been sleeping with my half-brother for four years."

Daphne asked, "Do I need to drive? I mean, are you feeling O.K.?"

"How the Hell do you think I feel? How would you feel if you found out you'd been fucking your half- brother all these years? And damn it, damn it to Hell, I enjoyed it!"

They rode in silence to Houston.

CHAPTER 18

Jon picked up the phone and dialed Bob Duggan's number at Hays. In some ways, this would be a great call, one that he had been eager to make. In other ways, this whole mess sucked, but better to be calling to say that in an awful lawsuit, he had won. And, Bob would be glad to hear that there wouldn't be any publicity for Hays.

"Bob Duggan, here."

"Bob, it's Jon Miller, with the Anderson lawsuit down here in Richmond. Got a minute to get an update?"

"Yeah, Jon, how's it going?" Bob sounded a little apprehensive.

"Yesterday we settled the suit, or at least have come to an understanding that Hays is harmless in the birth of the deformed children." Jon smiled; he had succeeded, even if he had learned there were a lot of sick people in the world.

"That's great, Jon, really great. I needed some good news. How did you manage to pull this off?" Bob asked, sounding very pleased.

"The confidential agreement that we will sign with Mrs. Anderson will not even contain this much information. Really I think that the best way to put it, in a very confidential manner, is that unbeknownst to their mothers, there are a lot of half siblings here in Richmond. Because it was unbeknownst to really anyone, some people got married and had children who really never should have."

"Whoa, wait a minute, what are you saying? It was incest that caused the problem?" Bob interrupted.

"Yeah, hard to believe, isn't it? And there may be more people out there with this gene who have no reason to suspect. Part of the settlement will be to fund some testing for some specifically targeted people." Jon took a deep breath, and then continued, "As much as I like working for Hays, and this really went our way, I hope that I don't run into anything this gothic again."

"Well, so all you have to do is get the final agreement worked out, do some billing, and then you can go back to doing whatever it is you small town attorneys do?" Bob asked, with a slight laugh. "Should I worry that the other party won't sign? Will it be a long negotiation?"

"No, the other party will sign. I think that they will sign almost anything, as long as the confidentiality is very high. And I don't see why it shouldn't be. There is nothing for Hays to gain by violating the confidentiality."

"Kinda funny, isn't it," Bob asked, "that in the beginning we were the ones who wanted the confidentiality, and even used the national security angle to maintain it, and it ends up that they want it as much as we do?"

"There's a lot of 'funny things' about this, but I guess you are right. We've come full circle," Jon answered. "I think I'll have the signed agreement for you to sign by next Wednesday. And I'll get Maureen to work out the billing and get that to you. And, if it's all the same to you, I won't be sending you much more than the bill for my monthly retainer for a while.

"Oh, while I've got you on the line," Jon said, "I think that Hays might consider sponsoring some Ph.D. work in Biology, probably at A&M, about any genetic problems in amphibians, for example, in the lower Brazos watershed. I'm pretty sure that it can't hurt, and if you call me again, it could be nice to have that sort of information."

"I got it. Always good to have the white hat information to put on, if we should ever need it. Did you have a professor in mind who might like to oversee this work?" Bob asked, knowing that, in deed, Jon would have just such a name.

"I've got some ideas," Jon answered, again with a smile, "and

I'll send them along when I send you the agreement. Talk to you next week, and thanks for letting me work the case."

"You're welcome. You did a fine job. Talk to you next week, Jon." With that, Bob ended the call.

Jon sat back in his chair. Well, he had to go get his uncle's wine out of storage, and he would draft the agreement. If he knew Mrs. Anderson, and he was beginning to, she wouldn't have to make a lot of changes so all he needed to do was get something down on paper and send it on. Then, on to billing.

In about an hour, Maureen had the first pass at the bill for Hays for him to review.

"Maureen, we forgot the two hours at the house of Mrs. Anderson's mother when I nearly got beaned with the Tiffany lamp and also the time for the phone call to the biologist at A&M. Please add those in to the bill for Hays. They're so happy they won't even notice. If I weren't so damn ethical, we could pad this with enough extra to get a new coffee maker and a small refrigerator to go under my desk. Ah! Another day, another case. 'That a man's reach should exceed his grasp, or what's a heaven for?'"

"Jon, can I get back to work? It's getting awfully deep in here." Maureen was smiling as she returned to her desk.

He was still enjoying his success when the phone rang. "Jon Miller."

"Jon, hi. It's Sandy."

"Hey, good-looking teacher. What's up?" Jon was surprised at himself by how pleased he was that Sandy had called.

"My dad's been having a good spell for a change, and I think I could leave for a week or so now that school's out. You think we could increase the population of Richmond by one for a week? Or is this a bad time for you?"

"No, it's a great time, come on over . . . you'll force me to clean up the house."

"Don't do anything drastic. Can you pick me up at Hobby tomorrow? Southwest Flight 1827 arriving at one ten. I will have missed lunch so you could take me to that little Mexican food restaurant I love, if it wouldn't be too much trouble," she asked in a coy manner.

"See you then."

"I love you. And I'll show you just how much tomorrow afternoon."

"I love you."

"Yes, sir. Flight 1827 is on time. The passengers will come down concourse A. Only ticket holders can go to the gate."

"Thanks," said Jon.

Sandy O'Rourke came down the concourse pulling a wheeled carry-on. Her red hair and tall silhouette made her easily visible. A broad smile filled her face as she saw Jon standing against the wall, wearing a Mexican sombrero on his head and a serape over his shoulder. He carried a single long-stemmed red rose.

"Senorita, you would perhaps like a 'leetle lonche?' Maybe a tortilla or an enchilada? Perhaps a taco?" said Jon handing her the rose.

"You clown! You know how I hate public displays of affection, but if you don't kiss me, I'll scream."

She didn't have to scream.

On the way to the car, Sandy asked "How did you determine the cause of all the trouble in your case with that female lawyer from Houston?"

"Sandy," Jon said laughingly, "we have a non-disclosure clause in the settlement. So being an ethical bastard, I can't tell you. Of course, there is a loophole. In Texas in the eyes of the law, a man and wife are considered one person . . . so if we were married, I could ethically tell you because I just agreed not to tell another person. So if I tell you, there are two alternatives: You can marry me or I'll have to kill you. What'll it be?"

"Oh Jon, you never give up, do you?"

"No, that's part of what you love about me."

"I accept your conditions. Tell me!"

"Does that mean you've decided to marry me?" Jon asked with disbelief written all over his face.

"I didn't say that! I haven't decided which of the alternatives to select. But when I've decided, I'll let you know. So you can go ahead and tell me."

"O.K., wiseass, you win. But it's one or the other," said Jon. Sandy laughed.

"You know I'm a big mystery fan. Sherlock Holmes was obviously the best except for maybe his brother Mycroft. Anyway, as Sherlock says in 'The Sign of the Four,' 'Eliminate all other factors, and the one which remains must be the truth.'

"Chromosomal changes can be brought about by a number of things. We could rule out irradiation by history. We know of no viral epidemic which affected them all. The material from the plant caused no chromosomal abnormalities in the cattle that died. I had the vets at A&M do an analysis on the specimens that they had kept of the dead cattle.

"The only remaining factor was inheritance. The doctor was the only common thread. When I saw the red checkmark on the medical folders and found out what it meant, I knew the truth. I only needed Dr. Richter to confirm it." Jon preened a little in light of Sandy's approval.

"Oh, another thing I was wondering about," Sandy continued as they made their way across the parking lot toward Jon's T-bird. "When you moved the records to the wine storage, you said that you left one piece of paper in the boxes in your office. What happened to that piece of paper? Did you write something on that piece of paper?"

"Well, since the boxes weren't bothered, I guess I overreacted. You sure know how to bring me back to earth," he said. He stopped, turned her toward him, and kissed her soundly. "I wrote, 'Mrs. Anderson, I presume,' on pieces of paper and stuck them in each empty box." He grinned guiltily. Sandy couldn't tell if it was about the case or about the kiss. She wasn't sure she cared.

"O.K., good Mexican food here we come," Jon said, as he settled Sandy in the car and put her bag in the trunk.

After a leisurely lunch, Jon said, "Could I show you off?"

"What are you talking about?" Sandy asked.

"Well, tonight's choir practice, and I'd like to let people meet you and let you meet some of them. So if you wouldn't mind too much, let's go sing."

"If we can have some quality time together without anybody else around after that, I'd love to meet your choir friends. No quality time, no choir," Sandy said playfully. She was flattered that Jon wanted her to meet his friends.

"How you put my thoughts into words, lovely school teacher. I think I've just been propositioned," he said with a wolfish grin. He had already planned to take Sandy by his house, but her suggestion had really motivated him.

"You're damned right, Sir Shyster."

"Folks, I'd like you to meet a nice school marm from New Orleans, Miss Sandy O'Rourke. You guys be on your best behavior, I don't want to run this one off."

Everyone came over to Sandy and introduced themselves, making wisecracks about Jon. It was a 'tough room,' but Sandy soon had them eating out of her hand. She was asked to join the sopranos for the practice, but she only agreed when the choir director assured her that she wouldn't have to sing on Sunday morning. "Not that any of the rest of them can actually sing, but you won't even have to sit in the choir loft with us if you don't want to," he said.

Bob Clark, the biologist, was a late arrival and the last to greet Sandy. "Jon," he said, "I just pulled this off the internet for you this afternoon. This web site claims proof that the deformities in frogs and other amphibians are caused by trematodes, small parasitic flatworms. Some professor is doing some experiments to prove that trematodes can be introduced into tadpoles and cause similar problems. So, maybe it's not pollution. Take that, Mr. Nader. Doesn't help the frogs much," he said smiling.

EPILOGUE

All the parties to the agreement have kept their word. Emma notified all those involved in the suit only that it had been dropped. The Coleman Foundation, Emma's father's foundation, evaluated all the red-checked folders finding only two more individuals with an abnormal gene. Every one with an abnormal gene was informed of the consequences and told that the cause of the abnormal gene was unknown. Hays Chemical was completely exonerated.

Maureen now has to wear a sweater all summer in the coldest office in Richmond.

Emma and Bill Anderson announced their divorce, but Emma was right, the church didn't have any problems giving them an annulment. Bill has remarried and is teaching his adopted son how to throw a curve ball. Joey, age two, hasn't quite gotten the hang of it, but all parties enjoy practicing. Bill and his new wife expect Joey's sister or brother in about five months.

Emma now works as in-house counsel for a large pharmaceutical company. Daphne has returned to the monotony of the secretarial pool despite Grace's efforts to snag her permanently. Daphne never did receive an invoice from Dr. Singh, as she correctly had predicted. The Coleman foundation, which Emma heads, makes significant contributions to the healthcare of indigent children of Fort Bend County. Angela and Emma's mother are once again getting ready for the homecoming dance.

Jon and Cato have resumed running in the morning. Both are a lot less testy. Sandy has returned to New Orleans to care for her father. Jon has started calling her every night.

I, the LORD your God, am a jealous God, visiting the iniquity of the fathers upon the children unto the third and fourth generation of them that hate me, And shewing mercy unto thousands of them that love me and keep my commandments.
Deuteronomy 5:9, 10